ALANA OXFORD

Blue Skies

8N PUBLISHING

For
Mrs. Kelly and Monty
Jennifer Treece, Milton and Snowball
All my readers who need a little blue sky right now

Contents

Chapter 1

Wednesday, July 15

*P*atrice's sweaty hands lie listless in her lap while her boss, Tyree Dare, looked at her mockups for the brochure. Well, not only looked them over, but failed to be as impressed by them as Patrice was. Patrice was certain she'd be a contender for an excellence award with this one. How did Tyree not see that at all?

"Do you have any more designs? These aren't grabbing me. I'm looking for the wow factor and I'm just not seeing it." Tyree looked up at Patrice, as if more concepts would appear out of thin air.

"Mmm." Patrice's mind scrambled to put together a brilliant argument for why her designs were the perfect vision for the client's specifications. They'd wanted a family-friendly vibe for their new camper and RV line and that's just what Patrice had delivered. From her perspective anyway. Per usual, she came up with nothing persuasive to say in the moment. No doubt it would all come to her, as a perfect, impassioned soliloquy while she brushed her teeth before bed. Removed from the pressure of an uncomfortable situation, she'd wax poetic about how she was right and the reps at Gilmore Camping and RV would fall in love with her designs. However, sitting in Tyree's office, facing the imposing woman who had built her ad agency from nothing, the only thing Patrice could think of was her own sense of defeat.

Tyree took off her reading glasses and handed the mockups across the desk to Patrice.

"Listen, we're running with a tight deadline on this brochure. The national camper and RV showcase is only six months away. I'm meeting with the client next Tuesday to approve a design. I need this from you by Monday, at the latest."

Patrice nodded, her throat feeling thick and dry.

"You don't think anything is salvageable?" How she managed to get the words out was a mystery to her; her voice sounded dangerously close to tears, even to her own ears.

Tyree looked at the paper for a few painfully silent moments, then leveled her gaze at Patrice. "Let's just see what else you've got. By next Monday."

Tyree picked up her phone to talk to someone, anyone, more important or competent than Patrice. Devastatingly dismissed, Patrice gathered up her papers and walked from the office trying to keep her head high. She knew she didn't deserve the treatment Tyree was giving her. The designs were good. Patrice may not excel at many things, but design was definitely one area where she did. Well enough to land a graphic design position at Tyree Dare Advertising Advantage right out of undergrad. It was a tough agency with a stellar reputation. She hadn't become the head creative on the Gilmore account by being subpar, but she'd let Tyree get the best of her.

She plopped down at her desk and stared at the concepts in front of her feeling utterly numb. While she was in this uninspired state, Sydney, one of her co-workers, walked in to chat. Patrice didn't even notice.

"Hey." Sydney snapped her fingers in front of Patrice's face, making her blink back to the present. "I'm trying to compliment you and you look like you've gone comatose. You okay?"

Patrice tried to swallow, but her mouth had become so dry she coughed instead. "Sorry. I'm lagging today," Patrice croaked in a froggy voice.

"These are really good designs," Sydney said, possibly for the second time. She pointed to one of the concepts Tyree had just dismissed. "But this is the strongest of all."

That got Patrice to perk up.

"Right? Tyree thought all of these were awful."

Sydney put her hands on her hips and stared down at the mockups. "You're kidding me. Why didn't you tell her off? You clearly nailed it with this one."

"Thanks, but I'm not big on telling people off. I'm very non-confrontational."

Sydney made a sour face. "Don't I keep telling you you're not going to last long in this business if you let people push you around? You let someone walk over you now, the next thing you know, you'll be trampled into dust."

Patrice had been there long enough to see that the place was full of forceful personalities, but that had never been her way. Sydney did often encourage her to toughen up and stick up for her work. It was easier said than done though. She loved the actual work, and the paycheck, but she could do without the drama.

"I know you're right, but she's Tyree Dare. Her name's on the front of the building. It's hard not to second-guess myself in front of her."

Sydney shook her head. "Don't do that. Tyree talks big but sometimes she wants her employees to show a little fight. You know this is good. Push back. It's not like she's going to fire you for doing good work and defending it. She didn't get to the top of the game by letting go of her talent."

It seemed a lot more reasonable when Sydney said it. It was just so much easier to have someone else do the fighting. Especially when her brain went blank as soon as someone stressed her out. Still, she'd have to try harder. On another day though. She'd promised Tyree new mock-ups and she intended to deliver.

The transition lenses of her glasses darkened quickly as Patrice stepped onto the sidewalk with her dogs for an after dinner stroll. She appreciated being home again after the rough day at work. Mr. Muffins, her chocolate Pomeranian, was especially energetic. He tugged on the leash, his little legs a blur of brown motion. In contrast, his "sister," Dolly, the orange, poofy princess, pranced along with reserved decorum. Patrice took in the sight of her happy little furbabies and broke into a smile for the first time that day. She was so lucky to have the two fluffy cuties in her life. Even when things were stressful, she could always count on the two of them to cheer her up.

By the time they'd walked a block to the intersection, Patrice could already feel a sheen of sweat on her face.

"Whew. It's hotter than I thought," she muttered to the dogs.

Spending most of the day in the refrigerator she called a work-place could really mess with her sense of actual temperature.

Dolly glanced up, her lolling tongue seeming to agree with Patrice. Mr. Muffins paid her no mind. He was still straining at his leash to get across the road and enjoy a nice jaunt in the park.

Once they crossed the street, Patrice headed to the tree-lined path through the park. She should have put some sunscreen on her pale face and arms before they'd left the apartment. The hot sun was already beating into her delicate skin and she didn't want to get burned. If it was still this hot in the early evening, it must have really been a scorcher.

Covered by the shade of the towering oak and maple trees, the air was much more comfortable, even if Patrice already felt like a sweaty mess. The dogs didn't seem to mind though. They trotted along merrily. Mr. Muffins was still leading with gusto, while Dolly remained back, closer to Patrice.

Breathing in the leafy air, Patrice's mind let go of camper brochures and turned to the uncomfortable state of her shorts. She contemplated what it might be like to have a custom tailored wardrobe. Her waistline had expanded a bit after she'd taken the job at the ad agency two years ago. With 95% of her day spent in a chair, she found her size twelve shorts from last year uncomfortably tight. However, the new size fourteen she had on were a bit too large, and they felt like they were creeping unreasonably low on her hips.

Off the path to her left, Patrice noticed a guy sitting on a park bench. His head bowed over a book and an umbrella lay by his side on the bench.

Patrice looked up through the trees and beheld a bright blue sky with a sparse array of wispy white clouds. It didn't appear there'd be any rain in the forecast, but stranger things had happened.

Her waistband slipped a little lower, prompting Patrice to make a decision. In that moment, three things happened:

Patrice used her right hand, the one holding Mr. Muffins' leash, to tug up her shorts.

Mr. Muffins caught sight of something intensely interesting up ahead. It excited his fuzzy brown head so much that he shot forward.

Caught off guard, the leash easily pulled from Patrice's fingers and Mr. Muffins shot off barking as his leash trailed uselessly behind him.

"Muffins! NO!"

The words burst out without any thought of who might hear. The little dog bounded off, at full throttle, with no regard whatsoever for Patrice's horror.

Dolly stood beside Patrice, the pair looking after Mr. Muffins's rapidly retreating form.

Before Patrice could formulate the best plan of action, she noticed another fast moving figure in her periphery. The man from the bench had leapt up, dropped his book on the ground, and chased after Mr. Muffins. The man's legs pumped like Forrest Gump as he closed in on the little dog. At the crucial moment, the man dove, landing hard on his knees, and scooped the dog into his arms.

Finally, Patrice's brain kicked into gear. She picked up Dolly and ran to meet the man who had successfully apprehended the breakaway pup.

Both the man and Patrice were out of breath when she got to him.

"Thank you," she gasped. "I'm so sorry. Mr. Muffins, stop!"

Mr. Muffins thrashed around, barking, in the man's careful grip. Patrice didn't think he would bite, but he'd never been tackled by a stranger before.

"It's okay," the man panted. "I have a dog too. I know how it is."

At that, Patrice drew her attention from her squirming dog to the man who had captured him. He was dressed in grey cargo shorts and a blue and red striped polo shirt. His sandy hair hung in shaggy waves around his head. It wasn't overly long, but Patrice thought he could do with a trim. His tortoiseshell glasses framed his large, brown eyes nicely. He was rocking a stocky, dad-bod look, but it wasn't unappealing. His full cheeks were red from the sudden exertion of running after Mr. Muffins in the heat, but it worked with the sweet, babyish features of his face. It was one of those faces that made it hard to gauge an age range. He might be eighteen. He might be thirty. Patrice found herself hoping he was somewhere in the midrange.

"Here." Patrice held her hands out. "I can take him."

The man looked doubtfully between the still wiggling dog and Patrice's outstretched arms.

"His collar's not on," the man said simply.

Patrice looked at Mr. Muffins and realized he was, indeed, completely liberated from his collar and leash.

"How the heck did that happen?"

"Dog powers," the man replied. "They have their ways."

She couldn't dispute that. Patrice looked behind her in the grass to see where everything could have disappeared to.

"I've got him," the man said. "Want me to carry him to your car and you can pick up his leash on the way? Seems like a good job for four arms."

Patrice was still surveying the grass. She didn't notice how the man closed his eyes for a second after the four arms comment, as though trying to find patience with himself.

"Oh, we just live down the road from here. We walked."

The man clutched Mr. Muffins tight to his chest and got to his feet. Patrice noticed right away that his knees were all scraped up and grass stained from his rough landing. She winced in embarrassment that her dog had caused such a mess for the poor guy.

"Well," he said, oblivious to Patrice's gaze at his filthy knees. "I can carry him to your place." He paused and then his brown eyes grew wide. "I mean, if that's not creepy. Geez, I only meant I don't mind helping. I'm not trying to be a weirdo." He hung his head like a sad puppy. "No one's ever accused me of being a ladies' man," he added quietly.

Patrice pretended she hadn't caught that last bit. She didn't get any uncomfortable vibes from him at all. He reminded her vaguely of someone. An actor, maybe? Some celebrity? Not that that made him a non-creepy person. Catching her dog, when he could have remained uninvolved, scored him a base level of trust. That and the fact that he seemed a little socially awkward.

She made a snap decision.

"You're not creepy. I'm really grateful you caught Mr. Muffins for me. I don't know what I would have done if you hadn't stepped in."

He smiled. "Like I said, I have a dog too. I'd be devastated if something happened to him. I didn't even think about it."

"Well, thank you so much. I'm Patrice, by the way."

"I'm Seth."

A light bulb went off in Patrice's head. A young Seth Rogen. That's who he sort of reminded her of. Kinda cute, in a goofy

8

sort of way. She just hoped this Seth wasn't anything like the raunchy characters that Rogen often played.

"Seth!" she exclaimed, then clamped her mouth firmly shut, deciding it wouldn't be a good idea to mention the coincidence of the Seth similarities. He probably got that a lot.

"Nice name," she said instead. "Well, I guess I'll take Dolly to see about Mr. Muffins's leash and collar. Then, we can retrieve your book and umbrella and get these furbabies home."

Seth crooked an eyebrow. "My book and umbrella? How did…"

Now it was Patrice's turn to feel awkward.

"I noticed you reading just before this guy bolted. Um, you don't see many people with books in public these days. I thought it was cool."

Seth looked down. "Cool? Me? I don't get that comparison often…or ever."

Patrice started to retrace the path of Mr. Muffins's escape to find where his leash and collar had landed in the lush grass.

Seth followed along, both arms tightly clamped around Mr. Muffins, who was finally giving up on his struggle to break free.

"So, what do you do?" Patrice asked, hoping his answer would help her get a ballpark estimate of his age.

"I'm an IT guy for a company in downtown Ann Arbor. I was lucky to get hired in as soon as I finished college and I've been there ever since."

Patrice nodded appreciatively. Stability, that was definitely cool. So was the knowledge that he was a college graduate. If he'd been at his job 'ever since' graduation, he could easily be in his mid-twenties. This was getting interesting.

"That's great. You must be really good at it."

Seth shrugged as much as he could while holding a dog. "It

might be boring to most people, but I like it."

"Aha!" Patrice spotted the leash and knelt down to pick it up. She examined the collar and was surprised to see that the buckle fastener had come undone. Maybe she'd been too preoccupied ruminating about work and too anxious to go for a walk that she hadn't secured it properly. Thank goodness he hadn't run off some other time when she didn't have a guy like Seth around to help out.

She wound up the leash and stuffed it into her pocket, causing the loose shorts to droop a little more. So what? She'd have bulging pockets and saggy shorts while Seth had grass-stained knees. They made a good pair.

"Let's get your stuff." Patrice gestured toward the bench. The umbrella was still sitting neatly on the bench, but the book was laying pages down in the grass.

Patrice grabbed the items, since Seth's hands were otherwise engaged.

"Is it supposed to rain today or something?" Patrice held up the umbrella.

"Oh." Seth chuckled nervously. "No. It's, uh, a weird personal thing, I guess."

"Okay," Patrice said, trying to figure out a way to swiftly change the subject.

"That didn't come out right," Seth frowned and tried again. "The umbrella was a gift from my best friend, Turner. It's actually really cool. Open it up."

Patrice glanced at the closed-up black umbrella in her hands and then at Seth to see if he was joking.

"For real," he urged. "It is cool."

"Isn't it bad luck to open an umbrella when it isn't raining?" Seth screwed up his face while he racked his brain for a reference to such things. "Nope. Nothing about not raining. I think it's only supposed to be bad luck to open an umbrella in the house."

"Oh yeah. That's what I was thinking of." Heat rushed to her cheeks thanks to her mistake. Luckily, they were already red from the heat so it wasn't noticeable.

Patrice carefully opened the umbrella, like she expected a coil of pretend snakes to come shooting out of it, but then she saw what Seth meant. Although the outside of the umbrella was an unassuming black, the underside was patterned with a blue sky and fluffy white clouds.

"Hey." Patrice's smile grew as she held it over her head and looked up at the lovely fake sky. "That is cool. I've never seen an umbrella like this before."

"Right? Me neither. Turner was really good at finding unusual gifts. Probably a byproduct of being online all the time. Anyway, he gave me that for my twenty-first birthday. It came with a card that said, 'Life sucks. Make your own blue skies.'"

Seth smiled at the memory, but Patrice felt like she was missing something.

"That's kind of an odd thing to say on someone's birthday. He sounds...interesting."

"Oh," Seth cleared his throat. "He was diagnosed with a brain tumor when he was fifteen. He'd been through some things, so he had a different perspective on life. The blue skies part was an ongoing thing between us.

"When we were seventeen, he went to an out-of-state hospital for surgery. While he was gone, I painted his bedroom ceiling blue and found cloud decals to make it look like a sunny day."

Patrice examined Seth's face, impressed that he would think

11

to do something like that for a friend. Not only was he cute, he was a good guy, as evidenced by the fact he'd caught a stranger's dog, and now she saw a glimpse of his kindness to an ailing friend.

"That's amazing," Patrice said. "So you started the blue skies thing?"

"Oh no," Seth shook his head vigorously. "That was all Turner. He came up with that as his life motto after he got the initial diagnosis. 'I got a shit deal,' he said. 'I gotta make my own blue skies from now on. However long I got.'"

Seth's voice cracked a little at the end and Patrice could see that his nose and eyes were getting a little red.

"Sounds like you both went through a lot." It was obviously a sensitive topic for Seth, but she couldn't stop herself from asking, "How's he doing now?"

Seth smiled sadly. "Actually, today's the two-year anniversary of his death. When I was heading out, I just felt like bringing the umbrella. Kind of like having him with me today. Is that childish? Geez, I don't know why I said all that. What a downer. Sorry."

Patrice gently closed up the umbrella, the weight of it in her hands taking on the sanctity of a sacred object. She felt really awful now. Here he'd been at the park, trying to spend some time with the memory of his departed best friend and Mr. Muffins had ruined it.

"I'm so sorry," she said. "That's not childish at all. I can actually relate to that quite a bit. One of my high school friends was in a fatal car accident our junior year. She wasn't my best friend, like you and Turner, but we had some classes together and we'd hung out a few times. We did elaborate presentations together for French class. We were dorks like that. Whenever we had

12

a dialog to present, we went all out. Singing, choreography, the works. They were like mini-drama presentations." She chuckled at the memory.

"Anyway, when she died, I bought a bracelet with an Eiffel tower charm on it and wore it every day. It helped me remember her and it was a good reminder that another day isn't a guarantee. I still put it on from time to time."

Seth stared at Patrice in open-mouth incredulity.

She looked away quickly. Crap. She'd totally misread the conversation. Besides, they'd just met. She didn't usually talk about that, not that it was the sort of thing that just came up in conversation. It made people uncomfortable to hear about a dead teenager. They never knew what to say so she'd learned to keep it to herself.

"Sorry," she said. "That got dark fast."

Seth shook his head, sincere interest on his face. "No. I just don't meet other people who lost a friend so young too. I'm not depressed all the time or anything, but it changes you to go through a loss like that. Most people can't relate. If I ever mention Turner, it usually freaks people out and they change the subject as fast as they can. I'm sorry you lost your friend too. What was her name?"

"Mariah."

"Mariah and Patrice. French class superstars. Man, I would have loved to see something like that."

Patrice chuckled. "We had a lot of fun in French class. Sounds like Turner was pretty cool too. I like that blue skies theory."

"Me too. It goes with your philosophy."

"My philosophy?" Patrice drew herself up tall in surprise. What had she given away without realizing it?

"Yeah. You said another day isn't a guarantee. You can put

13

the two together. Tomorrow isn't guaranteed, so make your own blue skies."

Patrice cocked her head as an idea popped into her mind. "Maybe we could start our own business and make inspirational t-shirts. Think anyone would buy?" She could already see possible designs swirling around in her mind. That's just how her brain was wired.

"Argh!" Seth exclaimed.

Maybe it wasn't the best idea, but she didn't expect Seth to react so negatively.

"I think your dog hates me." Seth stared down, tight lipped, at the little dog in his arms.

A cold shudder of panic replaced the vulnerability of nostalgia. Patrice hoped that Mr. Muffins hadn't bitten Seth after all, but she didn't have to worry about that for long. The dark stain spreading down Seth's shirt gave away the new horror Mr. Muffins had inflicted on this poor guy, on the anniversary of his best friend's death too!

Her mouth fell open in horror.

"Oh my God!" she exclaimed. She couldn't find any other words to say about it. Not only had Mr. Muffins ruined Seth's quiet afternoon of reflection, now he'd stolen his dignity.

"Let's just get you back to my apartment so you can clean up." Patrice's cheeks flushed with shame as she hurried along to her building.

Seth nodded, looking dazed.

As they passed other people, Patrice and Seth pretended they didn't see the shock on their faces. Seth was quite a sight with his grass-stained knees and urine-soaked shirt.

It felt like forever before Patrice was fumbling to get her key in the door. As soon as the door swung open to her apartment,

Seth plopped Mr. Muffins inside and stood in the hallway with his arms spread, staring down at himself.

The neighbor's door began to swing open and, without thinking, Patrice grabbed Seth by the arm, yanked him into her apartment, and slammed the door.

"Sorry," she exclaimed. "I don't want to be a weirdo, but I couldn't leave you out there like that with my neighbor coming out. She's too chatty and irritating to put you through that. This is all my fault and I feel terrible."

"It's not your fault. It was just an accident. A small series of them." Seth, to his immense credit, tried to laugh, but it wasn't a very convincing sound.

Patrice looked Seth up and down. He was a stranger in her apartment, yes, but she couldn't send him away like that. She'd gotten him into this mess. It was her job to help him out if she could.

"I know this is unconventional, but why don't you take a shower and get cleaned up? I can get your clothes in the wash and we can have you on your way in an hour or two, tops."

Seth looked down at himself again. "Your boyfriend, or husband, isn't going to show up as soon as I get in the shower and kick my ass when I get out, is he? It seems like that would be the next logical step today."

Patrice shook her head vigorously. "No, no! There's no boyfriend or husband. We won't have any unfortunate mis-understandings like that."

Seth sighed in relief. "Good, because I would really like to take that shower, if you don't mind."

"Please do. Here, follow me."

Patrice ran to her linen closet and grabbed a fresh towel and washcloth, the dogs running around her legs the whole way.

They nearly tripped her up. She shooed them off down the hall, handed the towels to Seth, and pointed him to the bathroom.

"I have an in-apartment washer and dryer. If you want to dump your dirty clothes outside the door when you're ready, I'll get them going while you're in the shower."

Seth furrowed his brow and held up a finger.

"Sounds good in theory, but I don't want to be the strange naked guy hanging out in your bathroom until the laundry's done."

The absurdity of the situation and her quick mental picture of Seth naked caused her to laugh nervously.

"I know this keeps getting increasingly awkward, but I do have some men's clothes here that should fit you okay."

Seth raised his eyebrows. "Just in case some poor sap wanders by needing a shower? Did this little guy set me up?" He pointed at Mr. Muffins, whose dark, beady eyes watched intently from beside Patrice.

"They're my brother's!" she hastened to add. "He stays here sometimes when he's in town from college. He forgot a pair of lounge pants and a t-shirt last time he was over."

Seth looked dubious.

"They're clean, I promise. It won't be as strange as it sounds."

Seth sighed.

"My shorts are good enough. I don't think any pee got on them, but the shirt would be great."

"You got it. Let me grab that for you."

Patrice dashed into her office, which served as a guest room when her brother was in town. She pulled the shirt out of the dresser and took a sniff. It smelled like the wood of the drawer and faintly of fabric softener. She hoped that would put Seth's mind at ease about wearing it. She could understand, she was weird about used clothes herself, but given the circumstances, remaining fully clothed in a stranger's presence was the best option.

She returned to find Seth crouched in the hallway outside the bathroom. He clutched the washcloth and towel in one hand and was petting Dolly with the other. Mr. Muffins peered around the corner, snorting in quiet disgust from time to time.

"Muffins, get!" Patrice shooed him away from the hallway. He'd caused Seth more than enough trouble for one day.

"I don't know what's gotten into him today." Patrice handed Seth the shirt as he stood up again.

"Anyway," she continued. "I wasn't expecting visitors. Please excuse anything messy in the bathroom." Patrice racked her brain trying to remember if she'd left anything particularly embarrassing out in the open.

Seth smiled, taking in the way her brow furrowed as she worried about what he might discover in her bathroom.

"No worries. I grew up with two sisters. I've seen some things."

Patrice sighed in relief.

"Okay, cool. I'll leave you to it. I'll be chilling with the dogs in the living room. I'll get your shirt in the wash in a few minutes."

Seth nodded. "Thanks." He made a show of opening the bathroom door and Patrice hurried away, not wanting him to think she'd be hovering around like a creep while he got ready to shower.

She made sure to be out of the line of sight for the bathroom. Mr. Muffins and Dolly looked at her expectantly while she stood in front of the television killing time.

Eventually, she heard the bathroom door open and close, then the water came on in the shower. She waited another couple moments, to be sure, and then went to retrieve the shirt Mr. Muffins had so rudely soiled. Seth had folded it nicely so the wet part was facing up, not directly on the carpet.

Considerate.

Patrice took the shirt to the little laundry closet off her kitchen. She tossed it in and selected the "express wash" setting. It'd be a thirty-minute wash, then thirty to forty minutes to dry. He'd be clean and fresh again in about an hour.

With the shirt washing underway, Patrice shifted into hostess mode. An hour with a stranger, even if he was sort of cute, had the potential to feel like an eternity if she didn't come up with a quick plan. Now that she had a moment to think, she realized she was parched.

She headed into the kitchen and opened a cabinet to pull out some powdered lemonade mix and a pitcher. She stirred up a batch, added some ice cubes, and put it in the fridge to chill a little more before Seth came out.

Cookies would have made a nice pairing with the lemonade, but she didn't have any. Instead, she set to work slicing two Pink Lady apples, some cheddar cheese, and placing them on a serving tray with crackers.

The next step was deciding where to enjoy them. The dining table was a neutral space, but it felt strangely formal. She settled on serving their snack in the living room, but knew better than to set it out before she was ready to partake. Two pairs of beady eyes followed her every move, silently begging for a treat to sustain them.

Patrice topped off the dogs' water bowls with cold water and broke out a fresh chewy to keep them occupied during her snacks with Seth.

The water shut off in the bathroom and Patrice suddenly

wished she could run in there and apply a quick touch of lipstick or powder before he saw her again. That certainly wouldn't be appropriate. She and her dogs had made enough of a mess of his day without her bursting in on Naked Seth in her bathroom.

Ooh. Naked Seth. Now there was a thought. What? No!

She couldn't call him that! Even if it was true, which it definitely was. A cute, naked stranger was toweling off on her bath mat at that very moment. His toes were sinking into its blue plushiness just the way hers always did, she was sure of it. What kind of toes were they? Bulbous and round? Long and fingery?

She'd already seen his bare legs. From the knees down, anyway. What was above that? Did he have a hairy chest and stomach? Smooth, but for a few spare hairs here and there? Were there any secret scars? Tattoos that weren't readily visible?

Patrice was so busy visualizing what might be that she jumped when the bathroom door opened. She turned back to the counter and picked up the tray of snacks.

"Oh!" she exclaimed when she turned to face him lingering uncertainly at the entrance to the kitchen.

"Sorry. I didn't mean to startle you." His damp hair clung to his head and the sweet, floral, ultra-feminine scent of her shampoo and body wash wafted to her nose.

"You smell really good." She couldn't help it. She hadn't thought about him having to wash up with her perfumed soaps. Poor guy.

"It is nice, although it probably smells a whole lot better on you. Anyway, I'm meeting my sister and her fiance for dinner tonight. If I smell like a pretty girl, that'll give them something to talk about." He waggled his eyebrows like that whole idea amused him. Patrice couldn't help but notice that he'd said

19

'pretty girl.'

"You'll certainly have a story to tell them about today."

Seth ruffled his wet hair and pushed his glasses up.

"They probably won't believe me. It sounds pretty far-fetched, if you think about it."

"Truth is stranger than fiction. Besides, the proof is in the perfume." Patrice winced as the words left her mouth. The proof is in the perfume? Who talks like that? But Seth didn't seem to notice, or mind, her awkward comment.

"It is a good story. Even if they don't believe me."

Patrice suddenly felt self-conscious thinking of what Seth might tell his sister about her. She nodded toward the tray she was still holding to keep her mind in the moment.

"I made us a little snack. Want to join me in the living room for some fruit, cheese, crackers, and lemonade?"

She noticed how deeply brown his eyes were. So dark they were almost black, but they sparkled when she brought his attention to the snack.

"That sounds really good. Thanks."

Seth got comfy on one side of the couch while Patrice set out the tray on the coffee table and then ran back into the kitchen to get the drinks.

The dogs munched merrily on their new chewies and left Patrice and Seth in peace. Who needed cheese and crackers when there were perfectly good chewies full of peanut butter?

Patrice filled her plate and settled in safely at the opposite end of the couch.

Seth swallowed his first bite of cheese and crackers and kicked off the conversation.

"You have a lot of cool artwork around here. Are you an artist?"

Chapter 1

Patrice was pleased he'd asked such an insightful question.

"I am, but I don't do a lot of fine art anymore. I'm a graphic designer for an advertising agency. So I'm mainly doing digital art, not paintings like these."

Seth stood up to get a better view of the piece nearest to the couch. It was just a little watercolor of a lake she'd vacationed at with her family. It had made her feel so calm and peaceful to be there, she'd hoped she could capture a little of that magic to keep in the painting. She'd done it when she was only eighteen, so it certainly wasn't her most mature work. Still, she liked it enough to display.

"I think I've been to this place." Seth took a bite of apple and stared at the painting, lost in thought. "Yeah," he snapped his fingers as the name came to him. "It was in Oscoda. Right?"

Patrice swallowed her bite and stared at him in surprise.

"It is! You could tell that from my little painting? I can't believe it."

He peered a little closer at the painting and then sat back down on the couch, smiling at Patrice.

"Are you kidding? This is really good. We had a family reunion out there once, at Lake Huron. Then we went on a nature hike and discovered that little lake you painted. I forget the name of it. It was really pretty. I haven't thought about that place in the longest time."

"I was there for a family vacation too."

"What if we were both there at the same time? Wouldn't that be wild? We might have passed each other on the trail and had no idea we'd ever meet again."

Patrice took a sip of her lemonade to cover her pleased grin. She liked the idea of their teenaged selves running into each other. If it had happened, then it was like fate that they'd happened upon each other again at the park. Even if Mr. Muffins had peed on Seth.

"Do you always have such a positive outlook?" she asked.

"Me? Positive? I don't know about that. I might just read too many sci-fi and alternate reality books."

"Is there really such a thing as too many books?"

"I like the way you think." Seth picked up another cracker and some cheese and took a thoughtful bite.

Patrice grabbed an apple slice, for something to do as much as because she was hungry. How could she respond to that?

"Anyway," Seth cleared his throat a little awkwardly. "You sure there's no significant other who's going to come home and show me out?"

Patrice shook her head, quietly relieved that he was moving toward a flirty topic. "There's definitely not. It's more accurate to say I'm turning into a spinster."

Seth literally choked on his cracker. "There's no way!"

"Oh but there is," Patrice assured him. "Let's see, my last boyfriend and I dated for two years before he cheated on me and dumped me just before college graduation. It's a lot harder to meet people when you're not at school. I mean, I've been on a few dates here and there, but it hasn't led to anything. I think I may be on the path to becoming a crazy Pomeranian lady, but it doesn't sound half bad."

"Cheated on you? Was he blind and stupid or something? Man, that's terrible. I'm so sorry you had to go through that, but it does sound like a runaway, urine-happy dog is an upgrade from that jerk."

"Thank you." Patrice was touched by his reaction, and it bolstered her confidence too. He was definitely feeling an attraction to her too. This was going very well. "I'm definitely better off without him. Could have done without the cheating. I bet he's already done the same thing to that girl and maybe a few more by now. Ugh. What a mistake that guy was."

Mr. Muffins and Dolly had finished with their chewies and were curled up in their little dog beds for a snooze. They did a good job of keeping her from feeling lonely, but if she was being totally honest, she wouldn't mind having a boyfriend. Especially a good, non-cheating one.

"What about you? Good-looking employed man. Don't tell me there's not a girlfriend who's going to be pissed you were showering at another woman's place this afternoon."

"Ha! I'm just your typical nerdy computer guy. I like numbers and codes. Sci-fi books and movies. I don't tend to make much of an impression on people. Since Turner, I hang out with my sisters more than anyone else. Kinda pathetic, really. I'm like the fifth wheel. Julie's engaged now, and Caitlyn has a boyfriend. Really, I think they only hang out with me because they have to, not because they really want to."

Patrice put a hand on his arm.

"Stop. I'm sure they love hanging out with you. You're a lot more fun than you give yourself credit for, I bet. I'm having a great time with you, so there."

She pulled her hand back and looked away, in what she hoped was a shy yet flirty manner.

Seth's cheeks got a spot of pink in them and he picked up his glass.

By the time the washing machine beeped, signifying that Seth's shirt was clean, Patrice thought that was the quickest half hour of her life.

"Shirt's done," she said. "Lemme just pop it in the dryer. Want any more lemonade?"

"Yes please. I forgot how good lemonade is on a hot day."

Patrice took care of the shirt and came back to top off their glasses. "What do you usually drink?"

Seth rubbed his mouth like he was trying to wipe away the answer before he said it.

"I may have a bit of an addiction to Pepsi," he confessed.

"Pepsi? Really? I don't have pop all that often, but when I do, I'm more of a Coke girl."

Seth slapped his hands on his knees. "Of course. I knew this was going too well. I guess I might as well grab my wet shirt and go right now."

Patrice reached out and lightly touched the bare skin just above his knee. It was warm and soft and she felt a sudden urge to lean closer and touch even more of him, but she knew enough to behave like a human being.

"Stop," she said, in a dramatic, breathless voice. "Don't let Pepsi and Coke allegiance come between a budding relationship."

Wow. She'd already touched him unnecessarily twice and now she was throwing around the 'r' word. But she didn't want him to think he'd been friendzoned. From what he'd said, she assumed he wasn't active on the dating scene. He was funny, but there was a strong sense of self-deprecation. She wanted him to get the idea she liked what she'd seen so far.

"No?" Seth asked. "Are you really saying you could learn to…tolerate…a man who drinks Pepsi?"

Patrice had a flashback to the Naked Seth images that had flitted through her mind's eye. If that was any indication, she could do way more than tolerate him.

Patrice looked into his dark brown eyes, earnest even though he was joking with her.

24

"Who knows," she shrugged, reaching for another slice of apple. "Maybe you'll be able to woo me over to the dark side."

Conversation continued to flow freely until the dryer buzzer interrupted. She'd set the dryer for forty minutes, but it felt like only five minutes had gone by. Reluctantly, Patrice got up and pulled the perfectly dry shirt out of the dryer. She hesitated for just a minute, wondering if she should pretend it was still damp and put it back for another ten or fifteen minutes, but she decided not to.

Seth drained his second glass of lemonade and took the shirt.

"Okay then," he said, looking up at her from his spot on the couch. "I guess I'll change back into this and get out of your hair."

"You can stay longer." The words shot out of her mouth. Seth gave her a bemused grin so she added the less eager, "If you want."

Patrice's heart thumped in her chest, hoping he'd say yes. She may have a mountain of work ahead of her, but that didn't seem nearly as pressing as spending more time with Seth.

"This has been really fun, but I should get moving." He glanced at his smartwatch. "I still have to meet up with my sister and her fiance."

Patrice mimed smacking her forehead. "That's right. You did say that already. Sorry."

When Seth went back into the bathroom to change, Patrice got an idea. She ran to get her purse and pulled out a rumpled postcard.

Seth came out, dressed in his own clothes again, and Patrice pressed the postcard into his hand.

"Here. My friend Emily is doing a concert this Saturday. She's in an Irish folk band called Sisters of Erin. Even if that's not your thing, they're really good. My friends Ashley, Tim, and I will be there. You could bring some friends too, if you're interested."

Seth glanced over the information. "Sounds fun. I'll see what everyone's up to and maybe I'll see you there."

"Great. Well, have a good time with your sister and almost brother-in-law. Thanks again, so much, for catching Mr. Muffins. Sorry he peed on you, but it's been really fun talking with you."

"No problem. Maybe you can catch my dog sometime and we'll be even."

Patrice wanted to hug him goodbye, but he wasn't making any moves to get closer. She didn't have the nerve to go for it.

"Don't forget your book and umbrella!" She scooped them up and handed them over, enjoying the warm moment of contact when their fingers touched.

"See you around," Seth gave a little wave and walked out of her apartment with no further ceremony.

Patrice gently closed the door and breathed in the lingering scent of Seth in her soap and shampoo. That was an unexpectedly fun detour in what should have been a crappy day. She took a couple more breaths before the perfumy scent dissipated. Then she smacked her forehead in frustration.

"Why didn't I ask for his number?"

She turned back to the interior of her apartment and saw the dogs staring at her expectantly.

"Mr. Muffins," she narrowed her eyes and pointed at the little guy. "Why didn't you remind me to ask for his number?"

He yipped at her and turned in a circle, hoping she was asking if he wanted another treat.

Well, she couldn't deny him when he was being so cute. She

walked back into the kitchen to get one more small treat for Mr. Muffins and Dolly. She may not have gotten Seth's number, but at least she'd invited him to Emily's concert. Now she just had to get through the week, create a new and brilliant mockup for Tyree, and hope Seth would show up at the concert. No problem. Right?

Chapter 2

Saturday, July 18

*T*he upside of having so much work to do was that Patrice spent the rest of her workweek in a frantic haze of forced creativity. It didn't leave her with much time for daydreaming about Seth or kicking herself for not getting his number.

By the time Emily's concert rolled around, Patrice was happy to leave behind thoughts of work and analyze the content of her closet instead. Still, she would have liked to convince the butterflies in her stomach to fly elsewhere.

"He's probably not going to show up," she said matter-of-factly over the phone to Emily. "My dog peed on him and he humored me while I washed his shirt. Why would he come? He's not going to."

"Patrice. Breathe!" Emily instructed. "Stop being silly. He'd be a jerk to pass up this invitation. He rescued Mr. Muffins for you, didn't he? That was chivalrous. A chivalrous guy isn't likely to stand you up."

Patrice fingered a blue halter dress she'd bought for a cousin's wedding the previous summer. "Well, it's not like it's an official date or anything, and he didn't ask for my number either. Maybe he wasn't interested at all."

"Stop it. I think he'll come, but if he doesn't, it's not the worst thing, right? It was just one hour."

"Maybe closer to ninety minutes with the park time included."

Emily laughed. "Of course. Ninety minutes. Anyway, my advice is to wear that black sleeveless top of yours with the red skirt. In the unlikely event that he doesn't come, at least you'll be looking hot if the real Mr. Right happens to be there."

Patrice scoffed. "Yeah? Is there suddenly going to be a gathering of hot, single guys at this show?"

"Mark my words, you're going to go home happy tonight." Emily sounded absolutely certain.

"I appreciate the support." Patrice slipped the black top off its hanger. "But could it be possible you're just optimistic because this is your first gig in a new venue?"

Patrice could hear the smile in Emily's voice when she replied.

"It is pretty wonderful, isn't it? We're going to rock this pub and this could be the break we need for the word to get out. Then Sisters of Erin can be my full-time gig instead of a side hustle. Fingers crossed!"

Emily's excitement was a perfect antidote to Patrice's nerves.

"I've got my fingers crossed for you too. You'll show 'em tonight, Em. Thanks for the outfit advice. I'll let you go get ready. See you there!"

Patrice finished putting herself together for the hypothetical non-date that might happen.

After shimmying into the outfit Emily approved, Patrice

headed to the bathroom sink to try and work some magic with makeup. Nothing too wild, not that she was much of a makeup artist. However, she could do a decent cat eye or a nice smokey lid.

The dogs followed her and sat just inside the door to keep an eye on the situation. Patrice appreciated the support of her furry little shadows.

She set her glasses on the counter and leaned in the necessary two inches from the mirror for her nearsighted eyes to see what she was doing. She opted for a classic smokey eye and the red lipstick that matched her skirt. She put her glasses on and stepped back to admire her reflection, twisting to scope out her backside too. The flared knee-length skirt hung nicely, even though she suspected she'd been a touch slimmer the last time she'd worn it.

"Well, what do you guys think?" Patrice twirled around for the dogs to get a good view of the full effect.

Mr. Muffins blinked his eyes blankly.

"Nevermind, Muffins. This is girl territory. What do you say, Dolly?"

Dolly cocked her head, as if really assessing Patrice's overall look. Finally, her mouth lolled open and she looked like she was giving a huge, doggy smile of approval.

Satisfied that she looked chic enough for the occasion, but still like herself, she checked the time, got the dogs crated, and left.

The closer Patrice got to the pub, the faster her heart beat. She had to keep a conscious effort to lay off the gas pedal. Apparently, her nerves manifested as a lead foot.

Having arrived safely, Patrice stepped out of her car and tried to inconspicuously scan the parking lot for any sign of Seth. Of course she didn't see him there. If he came at all, he wouldn't show up at the exact same time as her. Now she was just being ridiculous.

She did her best to take deep breaths as she walked into the pub. If she was going to get through the night, she needed to be calm. There was no guarantee Seth would even come. If he didn't, she needed to remember she was actually there to support her friend. This was a big night for the Sisters of Erin. They'd done a few small private engagements, but this was their first pub gig. This was a chance for the general public to hear them for the first time, and hopefully, fall in love with their music. Emily wanted this so badly and Patrice wanted it for her. Emily had been a driven musician ever since Patrice met her in fourth grade. She deserved this chance and Patrice had to be supportive of Emily first and foremost. Seth would just be the icing on the cake. Although, he seemed like he could be the cake itself. A humble spice cake. With cream cheese frosting. Unassuming. Not necessarily the sort of cake that popped into your mind as something you desperately wanted, but once you had a taste, you couldn't get enough.

"ID please, miss."

Patrice stopped abruptly as the bouncer stepped in front of her. Right. She was going to Emily's show. Not craving Seth cake. Seth cake? Really? What in the world was wrong with her?

She dug her ID out of her purse and showed it to the bouncer. He nodded and let her through.

Once she stepped into the pub, which prided itself on being authentically Irish, Patrice began to loosen up. The vibe was very cozy and fun and the air was charged with a palpable excitement. Maybe it was just Emily and the rest of the ladies who were pumped to show this place what they could offer, but Patrice really felt like something big was going to happen.

A quick sweep of the place revealed Emily standing to the side of the little stage with her bandmates, Clara, Lake, and Rose. They were crowded behind a little merch table they'd set up, just in case their dreams came true and they inspired a group of new fans.

Patrice made a beeline for the table and Emily came out to greet her with a hug.

"You look gorgeous in this," Emily said. "You're going to blow Seth's mind when he sees you."

Patrice's heart fluttered, betraying how much she wished he'd come. She hoped he wasn't at home thinking about what happened and deciding he didn't want to see the woman whose dog had peed on him.

"I see you worrying," Emily said, waving her hand in the direction of Patrice's face. "What's going on here?"

Patrice shook her head, not wanting to make the night about herself when it was such a big deal for Emily and the band.

"I'm fine. Let me see what you've got here." Patrice leaned over to examine the contents of the table.

Even though Emily's bandmates knew Patrice, Lake took the opportunity to go into saleswoman mode.

"Glad you asked," Lake said, stepping forward to hawk their wares as best she could. "Here we have a postcard detailing where and how you can download our music online. You can also check out our website and sign up for our newsletter to keep up with future shows. We also have some lovely Sisters of Erin stickers, perfect for decorating your car or anything else that needs a little flair. If CDs are your thing, we have some of those, which we're all too happy to autograph for you, and, of course, some t-shirts to show your Sisters of Erin pride wherever you go!"

Patrice smiled. "Good spiel, Lake."

"Thanks. I just figured I'd warm up. You already have all this stuff anyway, don't you?"

Patrice took a good look at everything. Yes. She did have it all, but she was in a generous mood. It was their first big gig, after all. She wanted to start them off right.

"I do, but you can never have too many stickers, can you?" She pulled out some cash and exchanged it with Lake for a few more stickers.

"Thanks. First sale of the night."

"May it be the first of many." Patrice tucked the stickers in her purse and looked up at the stage. It had a simple black backdrop, too small for a curtain in the front. The instruments were set up and ready to go, along with four microphones. Between them, the ladies played fiddle, bodhran, flute, tin whistle, accordion, and guitars. They were each extremely talented musicians in their own right, but together, Patrice thought they were on a completely different level.

Emily linked her arm with Patrice's and steered her away from the merch table.

"You've seen that old stuff a hundred times. Stop worrying. Mr. Muffins is a universe whisperer. He's got your best interests at heart."

"So you're saying my life is orchestrated by a spoiled Pomeranian?"

Emily raised her eyebrows with a sly grin on her face.

"Okay, don't answer that," Patrice laughed.

Patrice caught sight of a familiar form out of the corner of her eye. Not Seth, but her friend Ashley with her husband,

Tim. Patrice, Ashley, and Emily had roomed together in college, effectively cementing their friendships for life. Patrice and Emily had stood up in Ashley's wedding the previous summer.

The friends exchanged hugs all around. Patrice got so caught up in the excitement with her friends that she was a little surprised to feel a tap on her shoulder.

"We meet again," Seth greeted her, eyes darting around shyly.

"You came!" There was no disguising the enthusiasm in her voice, but the huge smile that spread over Seth's face indicated that he didn't mind at all. This time, she went for it and greeted him with a quick, friendly hug.

"Of course," Seth said while hugging her back. He was a really great hugger. She liked the sensation of her voice so close to her ear. "It sounded fun. Plus, I thought it'd be a nice change to hang out with you in normal circumstances."

He pulled away and smiled at her again. "You look beautiful."

Patrice looked away and smoothed a stray hair behind her ear. "Thank you. You look great yourself."

She did think he looked awfully cute. He wore a pair of black jeans with a green and blue plaid button down shirt.

"So you're Seth!" Emily exclaimed, jumping right in with a handshake. "I'm Emily, best friend of Patrice and member of Sisters of Erin, which you'll be enjoying tonight. So good to meet you!"

Bemused smile on his face, Seth caught Patrice's eye for a moment before turning back to Emily.

"I see my reputation precedes me. Hope I live up to the hype."

Emily grinned. "Any man who would take a shirt full of dog pee for my friend is a living legend. I think you'll be just fine."

Seth laughed heartily. "It's not the superpower I would have chosen for myself, but it seems to be pretty effective anyway."

Emily introduced the rest of the band and Patrice introduced Ashley and Tim. With that out of the way, it was Seth's turn.

"You said to bring friends, so I brought my sister and her fiance. They went up to the bar to grab drinks first, but they're on the way over now."

Patrice followed Seth's gaze and froze. Of all the people to see tonight, there was Jeremy Carson. She'd never expected to run into him again. Not after he'd cheated on her and dumped her for the bimbo at the gym. How did he have the nerve to be walking straight toward her now? With a woman on his arm, no less! She was so horrified, she couldn't take her eyes off him, until he stopped just in front of her.

Seth gestured to Jeremy. "This is my sister Julie and her fiance, Jeremy. Guys, this is Patrice."

If Patrice had been holding a drink, it would have slipped from her hands and crashed on the floor. As it was, she just stared, open-mouthed, at Jeremy and Julie. The couple in front of her. The couple that Seth had brought with him. Because they were his family.

Julie smiled, and Patrice could see the family resemblance right away. They had the same mouth.

"So nice to meet you!" Julie said warmly. "Seth told me the whole story of how you two met. Glad you got your dog back. That would have been so sad if Seth hadn't been there to catch him!"

"Yeah." Patrice's head buzzed with the shock of the situation. A one-syllable response was as good as it was going to get.

"It's funny how you can meet people isn't it?" Julie beamed up at Jeremy and placed a hand on his chest. "We met at a weight training class. I was just a beginner and this stud here took me under his wing and showed me how it's done. Didn't you, sweetheart?"

To his credit, Jeremy shifted his stance and his cheeks colored slightly. He took a swig of his drink and handed Julie the other one he was holding.

"Maybe we should take a seat," he said.

"Honey!" Julie gave Jeremy a little tap on the shoulder. "You didn't even say hi to Patrice. Don't be rude."

Jeremy's lips moved, but Patrice wasn't really paying attention. She was too busy dying inside.

Of all the people Seth could be related to, his beloved sister had to be the girl Jeremy had cheated with? Patrice hated her and was content to keep on hating her for the rest of her life. Now that she was looking her right in the face, Julie looked cute and bubbly, sure, but she was the cold-hearted, manipulative monster who'd stolen her boyfriend with no qualms whatsoever.

This couldn't be happening.

Patrice put her hands to her temples.

"Are you okay?" Seth leaned in, his hand a whisper of a touch on her shoulder. She liked the feeling of his hand on her but her conflicting emotions were too much to process.

"Maybe we should sit down." She blinked her eyes a few times and then focused on the rows of chairs set out for the show.

Julie didn't seem to notice how Patrice's friends were looking at her fiance, or how he was pointedly not looking at them.

"Oh, you're not getting a migraine, are you?" Julie asked, her eyes wide with concern. "I get those out of nowhere myself. I have some pain pills in my purse if you need anything."

Patrice shook her head and plunked down in the closest seat. "I'll be fine, thanks."

Patrice was in the aisle seat, so Seth sat next to her, Julie and

Jeremy squeezing past them to sit on the other side of him. Ashley and Tim sat directly behind Patrice.

Ashley leaned forward and squeezed Patrice's shoulder. "You want me to take him out back and give him what he deserves?"

"No!" Patrice shot back, as quietly as she could. She didn't want to alarm Seth, but she had to get herself under control too.

Ashley leaned back in her seat and Seth tried to take up the mantle of small talk.

"It's so cool your friend's a musician. You're a talented artist and I've heard you're a really immersive French-dialoger. I'm going to have to up my creative game. I got the top score at Skee-Ball once but that's not quite the same."

Patrice knew she was supposed to laugh at Seth's little joke, but the best she could do was a smile that probably came out more like a grimace. Considering that all her brain could think was, "OH MY GOD JEREMY IS ENGAGED TO SETH'S SISTER!" a grimace didn't seem like that bad a response.

Luckily, she didn't have to worry about conversation because Emily and her bandmates took the stage.

Patrice didn't hear the intro, her thoughts were too loud. All she could think was that Seth was going to be brother-in-law to her cheating ex! If she continued seeing Seth, she'd be with the brother of the woman who'd stolen her man. And he was close to his sister. It's not like she'd never have to see Jeremy and Julie again. It would be an ongoing relationship. For life.

But that wasn't even all that was horrible about it. Was it even worse that she'd been with a man who was now with Seth's sister? Marrying her! She knew intimate things about Jeremy. She'd met his family, for goodness sake.

What if, even though this was a really huge if, she and Seth were to fall in love and get married? She would actually become related to the man who'd humiliated her. Having her cheating ex-boyfriend for a brother-in-law? It didn't bear thinking about. It was unthinkable. In fact, it was making her sick.

As the band finished their first song, Patrice leaned over to Seth and whispered, "I just need to run to the restroom. I'll be right back."

"Sure," Seth answered, but she'd already jumped up and hurried away.

Patrice wanted to splash cold water on her face, but she didn't want to ruin her makeup and come out looking like a depressed clown.

She was just staring in the mirror when Ashley burst in.

"Are you okay?" Ashley asked, rushing over to put her arm around Patrice's shoulders.

"No, I'm not," Patrice admitted. "I never thought I'd have to see Jeremy's lying face again and now he's going to be Seth's brother-in-law? This is possibly the cruelest trick of fate I've ever heard of!"

Ashley paused, not quite sure what to say.

"Well," she finally began. "What do you want to do?"

"I really liked Seth," Patrice said, trying to stop her eyes from filling with tears. "I know I just met him, but I felt like we clicked, you know? But how can I start going out with someone who's going to be around Jeremy for the rest of his life? They probably even like each other! Argh! This is a disaster!"

Ashley patted Patrice's back as soothingly as she could.

Patrice's eyes grew wide as a new thought popped into her mind. It was like she was playing a game called 'One hundred worst case scenarios for your life.'

"Ashley, if Seth and I had kids, Jeremy would be their uncle!"

She had a vision of Jeremy bouncing her hypothetical children on his knee.

"No, no, no. I can't do this."

Ashley frowned and gave Patrice a squeeze. "Now that's a truly awful thought. Well, better to find out now before you'd gotten too invested in Seth, right? It sucks, but you're right. No one could be expected to put up with a situation like that. Let's just get through the show, support Emily, and then it'll be over. Okay?"

Patrice nodded. It would be awkward and horrible, but she could do that. Now her focus had changed. Her evening wasn't about the chance to see Seth again, it was just about supporting Emily. Then getting the heck out of there!

The pair returned to their seats.

The worry in Seth's eyes were like daggers to her heart. She didn't want to see him look like that. Her traitorous mind reminded her that Naked Seth had been in her apartment and how excited that had made her. She'd looked forward to seeing him here all week, and now he was right next to her but totally off limits. She couldn't believe her bad luck.

Her thoughts were interrupted by Emily launching into a scorching fiddle solo. She was so good that the crowd rose to their feet, whether they could dance a gig or not. They clapped and whooped and danced anyway.

Despite the situation, Patrice couldn't help but get caught up in the music too. Emily and the band were really playing their best. Emily was like another creature entirely when she played. Barely human, mostly instrument.

Seth turned to Patrice and did his best to dance along with her, although they both did more clapping and hopping than actual dancing.

When the song ended, everyone cheered. Patrice felt sweaty but so happy for Emily as Seth caught her eye and smiled.

He leaned in to be heard over the cheering and continuous applause. "I suck at dancing, but that was fun. Your friend is amazing."

Patrice nodded as she caught her breath. "Yeah. She really is."

The band took a break to rest a little before the next set. Without the music to focus on, the imminence of small talk filled Patrice with dread. How different tonight was than sitting with Seth in her apartment just days ago.

Julie leaned across her brother to talk with Patrice.

"Your friends are incredible!" she gushed. "I'm so glad you invited us. I'm going to download their albums right now!" She wasn't bluffing. She pulled out her phone and got right to it.

Of course, Patrice was happy for Emily's band to make an album sale, but she couldn't stop the images that were flooding her head: Jeremy with Julie while Patrice sat in her dorm watching movies with the girls or doing her classwork. It wasn't a nameless, faceless man-stealer anymore either. It was Julie. Seth's sister. Julie with wavy brown hair like her brother. With a warm and sweet round face and smiling brown eyes. She didn't look like the devil, but Patrice knew otherwise. Julie'd had no trouble taking up with her boyfriend two years ago and now she was even going to marry him.

She was starting to feel sick again.

"Can I get you something from the bar?" Seth asked.

At first, her impulse was to decline, but she reconsidered. It might be easier to get through the rest of the evening with a drink in her.

"Yes please, I'll have a rum and Coke."

Seth got up to join the crowd at the bar and Julie made her

way to the restroom, leaving Patrice two empty seats away from Jeremy. He didn't waste any time sliding into the seat next to her.

"Hi Patrice." Her name sounded like marbles in his mouth. It no longer belonged there and she didn't like hearing it. "What a surprise running into each other like this, huh?" He tried a friendly laugh but Patrice just gaped at him.

He cleared his throat. "You look great. How have you been?"

"Why are you doing this?" Patrice hissed. "We don't have anything to say to each other."

Jeremy's shoulders sagged. "Listen, I know I really did wrong by you in college. I'm genuinely sorry for that. I didn't handle any part of that situation maturely. I know that now. I don't expect you to ever forgive me, but I have wanted to apologize to you. Never expected there would be a chance like this."

Patrice glanced over her shoulder, hoping Seth hadn't returned to overhear any of this. She saw he was still waiting patiently while bolder, drunker people managed to push in front of him.

She turned back to Jeremy, still fighting to push back her shock at the whole situation.

"Well, looks like it all worked out perfectly for you both. Good thing you didn't let me hold you back. When's the big day?"

Jeremy may have made some terrible mistakes in his past, but he was smart enough to recognize the dangerous edge of a seething voice. "Patrice, we don't have to do this."

"Do what?" she asked. "I asked a perfectly reasonable question. When is your wedding? Or have you not set a date yet in case something better comes along?"

Jeremy rubbed the back of his neck. "October eighteenth."

"Fall wedding. Sounds cozy."

"That's the plan," Jeremy said. "Who knows. Maybe you'll get to see for yourself."

Patrice felt like a cartoon with her eyes popping out of her head.

"With Seth, of course," Jeremy added quickly.

"This is only the second time I've ever seen him. That's a far cry from wedding date potential."

Jeremy shrugged. "He's a good guy. A little out there, but really nice. He was so excited about you after you guys met. Jules said she's never seen him like that before."

Another horrifying thought crossed her mind.

"Did you both know it was me right away? There aren't exactly a ton of Patrices running around."

"No, no, no," Jeremy assured her. "He didn't mention your name, at least, not to me. Just said that he'd met a really great girl at the park. Anyway…" he looked down at the empty glass in his hands. "Julie doesn't know."

Patrice wasn't sure she'd heard that right. "Julie doesn't know what?"

Jeremy ran his hands over his face and sighed. "I don't really want to say this to you."

"Say it." Patrice leaned forward. She felt like they might be moving headlong into a trainwreck, but she needed to hear what Jeremy had to say.

"I never told Julie I was with someone else. She never would have given me the time of day if she'd known. She's a good person. Better than I was. Seth too. I hope this doesn't ruin anything for you. I wouldn't want to hurt you again."

"You have nothing to do with my life!"

Patrice could feel herself getting worked up. Who did Jeremy think he was? His thoughts had no impact on who she spent her time with. Her past anger was quickly resurrecting, awakened by Jeremy thinking he continued to hold any power over her after all these years.

"I'm sorry. That's not what I meant." Jeremy glanced up at Seth approaching and scooted back to his seat.

"One rum and Coke for you." Seth handed Patrice her drink with a little flourish that would have made her smile if she didn't feel so miserable.

"Thank you," she said, still conscious that Seth was a nice guy who hadn't done anything wrong. He was just, unfortunately, entangled with terrible people. "What did you get?" She peered at the glass in Seth's hand.

"Designated driver. I just got a Pepsi."

Patrice frowned. "I'm sorry. I would have just gotten a pop too if I'd known."

"No, that's totally fine. I wanted you to get whatever you'd like. Here." He raised his glass. "To a wonderful evening with delightful company."

"Cheers," Patrice said with as much enthusiasm as she could muster. Poor Seth. He had no idea what he was saying.

Julie came back from the bathroom and crouched next to Patrice.

"It's so cool you have a friend in a band! Do you get to follow them around when they travel?"

"They haven't actually traveled yet," Patrice said, trying not to imagine Jeremy and Julie making out at the gym while she was home wondering when Jeremy would call her. "They're planning to go to a folk festival in the fall. That'll be really exciting."

"Wow! That's great! There's so much hometown talent if we look for it. I'm so glad I found out about Sisters of Erin. They just got a new fan in me!"

"I'm glad you're enjoying the show." Patrice didn't want to be a jerk, but even if Julie hadn't known about her, it still wasn't fun to be face to face with the woman who'd successfully stolen her boyfriend. It's not like she wanted Jeremy back. By no means! She knew they weren't meant to be, but it didn't mean she wanted to be Julie's best friend. Or have Jeremy back in her life.

"I definitely am. It's so lucky your dog introduced you to my brother. It's like it was all meant to be!" Julie flashed another smile and went back to her seat. She had no idea she was trying so hard to ingratiate herself to her fiance's ex-girlfriend. Patrice took a big sip of her drink. If Julie knew the truth, she might not think it was such a lucky encounter. Would she even want to marry Jeremy if she knew she'd been the other woman when they met? It rankled that she did seem like a sweet person. In another circumstance, she would be very likeable. As it was, Patrice just didn't think she could do it.

Seth caught her eye and gave her a nervous grin that broke her heart. He was a kind-hearted, observant guy. Of course he'd figured out something was going wrong. He probably thought it was him.

Patrice raised her glass for another big swig. That rum better start doing something to take the edge off fast or Patrice was going to just die from the unbelievable situation.

Her only consolation was that they were at a concert and didn't have to spend the evening making small talk with each other.

The rum and music did a little to help Patrice get ahold of herself, but when the band was finished, oh boy.

Julie was so into everything, she jumped up and pulled Jeremy over to the merch table to spend more money and meet the whole band.

Ashley and Tim checked to see how Patrice was dealing with everything, but she knew she'd have to talk to Seth. She couldn't avoid it any longer.

Seth stood next to her, fidgeting, while their other friends dispersed.

"Hey, I'm glad you invited me to this. Would you want to go out with me again sometime? Maybe just us?"

Patrice took a deep breath. "Um, Seth. There's something I have to tell you."

Seth put his hands in his pockets and puffed out his cheeks.

"You got a boyfriend this week, didn't you? I knew it was too good to be true."

"No, Seth. That's not it." Even though she was about to let him down, she couldn't stop herself from resting her hand on his arm. Ignoring how good it felt to make contact with him, she made sure Julie and Jeremy were still occupied with the band and then let it out.

"Actually, do you remember how I told you about that college boyfriend of mine?"

"The ignorant cheater? I remember."

Patrice steeled herself and just said it.

"Well, turns out your sister is going to marry him."

Seth's face was totally blank until his brain started to connect the pieces.

"Jeremy is your ex? The one who cheated on you?" He looked stricken.

"Yeah. And Julie happens to be the girl he left me for."

"But...Julie?" He looked over at Julie and Jeremy. They were deeply engaged in conversation with Lake.

"Julie never knew about me. Jeremy just told me as much at intermission."

Seth ran his hands through his hair as he stared incredulously from Patrice to Julie and Jeremy.

"I told you I wasn't so good with women," he finally said, "but this is an all new low."

"I'm so sorry," Patrice said. "Seeing Jeremy here threw me for a loop, but then to realize he's marrying your sister, and who she was. Well, it's a lot to take in."

"I'd say so." Seth crossed his arms over his chest. "He's a cheater and now he's going to marry my sister! He's almost my brother-in-law!" He sat back down in his seat with a heavy thud. Patrice sat next to him.

"Yeah, that's all I can think about. My brain's been screaming that to me all night. It's a mess. I really like you, Seth, and under any other circumstances, I'd love to go on another date with you, but this is too weird for me. I'm sorry."

"Yeah. No, this is definitely uncomfortably weird. And now Julie has no idea what kind of man Jeremy really is. How can I tell her this?"

Patrice's eyes grew wide.

"No! Don't tell her that. She seems so happy. The thing with Jeremy was a couple years ago. Just forget about me and I'm sure those two will have a long, joyful, life together."

"But he's a cheater!" Seth exclaimed. "If he could do that to you, he could do it to Julie. There's a reason 'once a cheater, always a cheater' is a thing."

Patrice shrugged and looked helplessly over at Julie and Jeremy as they continued to laugh and talk with the band. Any rum buzz she may have had earlier was long forgotten now.

"I don't want to be responsible for ruining your sister's

wedding." Patrice's stomach flip-flopped at the mere idea.

Seth looked stricken. "You're not! Don't say that. It's absolutely Jeremy's fault. What he did to you and what he neglected to tell Julie. You're not responsible for any of that."

"But if Mr. Muffins hadn't peed on you, I never would have invited you here and no one would have ever known about Jeremy and me. Wouldn't everything have been better that way?"

Patrice and Seth stared at each other, hearts and minds racing.

"I…I don't know," Seth said quietly.

Patrice adjusted her purse strap on her shoulder. "Anyway, I should probably go. Maybe I'll see you at the park again sometime."

Seth raised his hand, like he wanted to stop her, but then didn't quite know what to do.

"I wish things hadn't turned out this way," he muttered.

"Me too."

Unable to take any more, Patrice turned and walked straight out to her car. She didn't dare go near Emily and the band. Emily would understand. They'd talk later.

Ashley and Tim were waiting for her outside.

"Hey!" Ashley hurried over. "What a horribly awkward evening. Are you alright?"

"Yeah. I just need to get home. The dogs need to be let out before bed anyway."

Tim put his arm around Patrice and gave her a brotherly side hug.

"Even though that was an unexpected blast from the past, I thought you handled it with a lot of grace."

"Thanks, Tim." Patrice rested her head on his shoulder for a minute, grateful to feel supported by her friends at such a crappy time.

"Let me know if you need anything," Ashley said. "Even if it's a three o'clock in the morning phone call."

"I will," Patrice assured her.

Once she made it to the solitude of her car, she crossed her arms over the top of the steering wheel and sobbed into them.

Maybe it was better to know early on that it couldn't work out with Seth, but it didn't make it any less hurtful.

Chapter 3

Monday, July 20

*P*atrice got through the aftermath of the concert as best she could. Monday dawned brighter and earlier than it had any right to, and she hurried into work with her new mockups to show Tyree. She'd used the rest of the weekend to channel her frustration into productive energy.

She took her stack of mockups and walked into Tyree's office. "Got a minute?" Patrice asked.

Tyree looked up from her computer and motioned for Patrice to sit down. "Let's see what you've got."

Patrice handed over the full stack of concepts, including the ones she'd shown Tyree on Monday. Tyree put her reading glasses on and carefully looked over every page.

Patrice sat in silence while her nerves jangled around like a fly trying to crash its way out of a window.

Finally, Tyree looked up and stared Patrice dead in the eye. "Tell me which one of these is your favorite."

Patrice took a shaky breath, feeling like she was standing before a judge and jury who wanted to find her guilty. She shuffled through the papers and came to one of her designs from Monday.

"Personally, I feel this is the strongest." She pointed to the design in the question. The one she felt could win an excellence in advertising award. The same one Sydney had singled out and told her to fight for.

Tyree considered the design and then looked back at Patrice. "And what is it about this one that makes it the strongest, in your opinion?"

"I think it exceeds the brief the client laid out for us. They wanted a family-friendly vibe to appeal to the broadest section of potential buyers so I took that idea and created a brochure the whole family could enjoy together."

"Mmm?" The open expression on Tyree's face asked for more. Given that she'd seen the same piece last week, and dismissed it, Patrice was still reluctant to defend it. Sydney may have given her a good pep talk, but she could feel herself shriveling under Tyree's no-nonsense gaze. Instead of letting herself crumble in the face of adversity, she suddenly remembered Seth admiring her artwork on the wall. He'd been so into it. He even recognized what she'd created. If he was sitting across the desk instead of Tyree, what would she explain to him about the brochure? The idea excited her and she decided to just talk Tyree through it like she would to Seth, rather than her boss.

Looking only at her mockup, she explained each and every design choice. Every rationale behind why she'd done what she'd done and how it met, or exceeded, what the client needed. When she was finished, she sat back in her chair, heart pounding with the excitement of what she'd created. After falling silent for a few moments, she finally looked up at Tyree.

Tyree looked back at Patrice with a pleased smile on her face. "So you do have a lot of passion behind this piece," she said.

"Yes, I do," Patrice agreed. "In fact, I feel so strongly about it that I think it could be a contender for the excellence in advertising award."

Tyree looked down at the papers and nodded thoughtfully. "I think you're right."

The words crashed over Patrice's head like a plate glass sheet. "You do?"

"Don't look so surprised," Tyree chuckled. "You've got some really strong work here."

"But you saw this same work last week and you hated it." Patrice was totally confused.

Tyree leaned back in her chair. "I never said that. What gave you that impression?"

"You said to create all new concepts. You didn't say you were willing to take any of these to the client. I thought that meant you hated them." Patrice hated to admit that she'd made a mistake, especially with her boss, but the concert had rattled her so much, she wasn't working with her usual protective walls up.

"Listen," Tyree said, leaning toward Patrice in a conspiratorial manner. "This is a tough business. You know that already."

Patrice nodded. Boy did she.

"You're a great designer, Patrice. That's what got you in the door here. What you still need to learn is that design isn't always what sells the concept to the client. It's the passion. I wanted you to show me your passion for the design so I could bring that with me when I present it to the client. But you know what? In this case, I think it'd be better if you did it yourself. You're coming with me to the Gilmore meeting tomorrow. You show them what you just showed me, and they'll be just as excited to sign off on this as you were making it."

"Wow. Thank you." Patrice didn't know what else to say.

Tyree gathered up the papers and handed them back to Patrice. "Just remember this," she said. "You don't have to wait for someone else to validate your good work. Own it, okay?"

"I will." Patrice took the papers and went back to her desk, feeling a thousand times lighter. At least until she went back home after work.

She had just settled in to watch a Monday night movie, sandwiched between the dogs on the couch, when her phone rang. Emily.

"I've been waiting for you to call me about what happened Saturday. I didn't want to push you, but I'm not waiting anymore. Are you okay?"

Patrice switched off her TV and let out a deep breath.

"Well, you know. I didn't need to see Jeremy, engaged to the woman he cheated with, but otherwise, I'm totally fine. Things went really well at work today. Turns out Tyree really liked that concept of mine too and she wants me to go with her to present it to the client tomorrow."

"Congrats on that. I'm excited for you, really, but what about Seth?"

"What about him?"

Emily grunted in frustration. "You were so excited to see him again! You were really into him. Now what happens?"

"I didn't really know him. What's an hour together in the grand scheme of life?"

"Patrice! Listen to yourself! Are you going to allow Jeremy to ruin your life all over again? Don't give him that kind of power."

Patrice sighed and absently scratched behind Dolly's fuzzy orange ears.

"I get what you're saying, but it's more than that. Don't you think it's sort of oddly incestuous? I mean, Jeremy and I were together. Now Seth's sister is going to marry him. How could I possibly be with Seth after that? That's like Jerry Springer level messed up."

"Gross," Emily agreed. "I hadn't really thought of it like that."

"Unfortunately, I can't stop thinking about it. Besides, say this ended up going somewhere. Jeremy could end up being my brother-in-law! At family events, I'd always be thinking that I used to be romantically involved with my brother-in-law. Could anyone stand a situation like that?"

Emily paused, taking this in for a moment before she spoke again.

"Well, does Seth really have to see his sister again? Plenty of families don't get together. Or he could just see his sister on his own time and leave you out of it."

"I'm not going to ask a guy to abandon his family after an hour of conversation. Seth is really close to his sisters. It's better to just let it go now and move on."

Both fell silent letting the impossible situation soak in.

"Well," Emily finally said, "That really sucks."

"Yeah," Patrice agreed. "It'll be okay though. There's other fish in the sea." Dolly huffed in her sleep as if she was scoffing at the idea.

"I'm sorry it turned out like this. Seth seemed like a really great guy." Emily's tone was somber.

"He is. He's just inextricably tied to the most humiliating part of my past."

"Through no fault of his own," Emily was quick to point out.

"No. But deeply tangled up in it all the same."

"You sure you're alright?" Emily's gentle tone made Patrice want to cry.

"I'm fine." She was surprised her voice came out stronger than she felt. It was silly though, wasn't it? Why did it feel like a bad breakup when she'd barely even known the guy?

She shook her head, hoping she could shake some sense into herself. Sure, it was totally easy to meet quality men now that college was in the rearview mirror and she worked with the same group of (mostly married) people day in and day out. Surely, she'd find someone else she clicked with, even though it hadn't happened yet. More fish in the sea. More dogs at the park. All that jazz.

Or it was all a load of crap and she was missing out on the best guy she'd ever met?

"Argh!" Patrice groaned in frustration. "I'm not fine, okay? I did really like Seth. I can't stop thinking about those adorable brown eyes and that sweet face of his. He's nerdy and kinda shy, but he has this confidence about himself anyway. And you know what?" She didn't wait for Emily to answer. "When Tyree was grilling me about my concepts, I was all ready to shut down, like I usually do when I'm stressed out, but suddenly Seth popped into my head. I wondered what would I tell Seth if he'd asked about my concept and I just talked about it like I would have to him. That's why I did so well. He helped me out again and he'll never even know it. Argh! Why did Jeremy have to cheat with Seth's sister? Of all the women in the world, why was it her? And why did it work out for them? I hate this!"

Dolly sat up, so concerned that Patrice was upset, she started barking. Mr. Muffins, also awakened from his slumber, jumped up on Patrice's lap and started licking her face.

"Sounds like everyone's upset," Emily said sympathetically. "Maybe you should talk to him again. There's got to be some way you can work things out."

Patrice scoffed. "Even if I wanted to, I never got his number and I don't even know his last name. It's over Emily. I just have to get it together and move on."

Patrice gave Mr. Muffins a one-armed hug and got him settled on her lap. Not to be outdone, Dolly squeezed in next to Mr. Muffins and rested her chin on his back. Even though it wasn't exactly snuggling weather, Patrice appreciated the solidarity from her babies.

"But Seth was so-"

"Stop it!" Patrice used her firm voice. "Seth 'was so' a whole lot of wonderful things but I'm trying to get over it, Em. Let's not talk about it anymore. Tell me about the gig. It looked like you had a lot of interest at the merch table after the show. What's next for Sisters of Erin?"

Her subject change was successful and they finished the duration of their conversation talking about the new opportunities in store for Emily and the band. It was good to have something positive to think about instead of the sting of her missed opportunity with Seth. When she ended the call with Emily, her conversation with Seth popped into her head uninvited. Specifically, the part when he told her about his friend, Turner, and the umbrella. Turner said sometimes you had to make your own blue skies. Maybe that's exactly what she needed to do. Even though it felt stormy and uncertain, she could get past it. She'd have to focus on something else and make some goodness come from it.

She stroked the heads of her snoozing companions. "Yes, I'll have to make my own blue skies." She wasn't going to get over Seth by sitting around dreaming about him. She had to take action, just like she had with the Gilmore brochure.

Dolly made a little sleep woof and her feet started to twitch like she was dreaming of chasing a mouse. Dolly and Mr. Muffins may not be able to help her scheme, but she didn't mind. An idea was coming to her now and she was willing to run with it.

Even though she'd just gotten off the phone with Emily, she sent a group text to Emily and Ashley.

Patrice: Hey. I need to get into the dating scene. Know anybody worth setting me up with?

Emily: !!!

Ashley: I do!

Emily: Are you sure this is a good idea?

Patrice: I'm not going to meet anybody if I don't put myself out there, right?

Ashley: Right! I know a great guy!

Patrice: Ok then. Ashley has a winner.

Emily: Who is this guy you just happen to have on hold?

Ashley: He's a new guy at my office and he's soooo good looking!

Emily: Does Tim need to be worried?

Ashley: Ha. Ha. I'm married. Not blind.

Patrice: What's he like?

Ashley: The first thing you notice about Chris is how good he smells.

Emily: Too much cologne?

Ashley: He's into essential oils. But he picks good ones. None of that patchouli that makes you choke on its fumes.

Patrice was starting to get an image of this essential oils Chris.

She tried to keep an open mind, but she was worried he might be a little earthy for her.

Patrice: He's not going to think I'm gross and full of chemicals is he?

Ashley: No! He's not like that at all. He's really nice. A good team-player.

Emily: Ooh! A team player. That's hot, Ashley.

Ashley: Yeah? You got anything better?

Emily: …

Ashley: Give Chris a chance. I can talk to him tomorrow at work.

Patrice: He's not going to think this is weird, is he?

With the imminence of Ashley talking to this guy in less than twenty-four hours, Patrice was suddenly hit with doubt that her blue skies plan was well-thought out.

Ashley: No way.

Emily: How long have you worked with this guy? Why haven't we heard of him before?

Ashley: How often do we talk about my work?

Emily: Um.

Ashley: Exactly. He's been there for about four months.

Emily: So still the honeymoon phase.

Ashley: He made it through the ninety days probation period. He's all good.

Patrice: What does he do, exactly?

Patrice knew that her friend was an insurance agent. There were lots of different kinds of jobs this Chris could have at the office. She just wanted an idea of what they might have in common. So far, essential oils were not it.

Ashley: He's in the marketing department.

Okay, so she'd have something to talk about with that. Even

though she was in graphic design, it didn't mean she wasn't aware of all the marketing speak that went on around her in the company. She had to admit, they might have a little in common there.

An image of adorkable Seth with his dad-bod and friendly smile popped into her mind. It gave her heart a twinge of longing but she put that away and focused on the new blue sky at hand. Chris the marketing, essential oils guy. If Ashley said he was a potential match for her, she trusted her. It's not like she'd been successful on her own.

Patrice: Sounds great. Let's go for it.

Emily: Essential oils. You sure about this, Ash?

Ashley: She'll see. Trust me.

Patrice: I do. Let me know what he says tomorrow. Looking forward to it!

With that settled, Patrice put her phone away, hoping she'd done the right thing.

The next day, Ashley wasted no time getting back to Patrice.

Ashley: Just talked to Chris. He's in! He gave me his cell # if you want to text him & work it out.

Patrice got the text while she was at work. The news sent a shiver down her spine, but it was more like the shiver that came from watching a horror movie, rather than, say, contemplating Naked Seth behind the bathroom door. But she needed to stop thinking about Naked Seth and start focusing on a viable future plan. So texting with Chris was next on the list.

Patrice: Cool. Send it over. I'll text him after work.

Ashley replied quickly with the number.

Chapter 3

Patrice couldn't help but think how easy it was getting Chris's number, but she still didn't have Seth's after she'd seen him two times. Not that it mattered. She didn't need Seth's number for anything. Why was she even thinking about such things? She had Chris's number now. That was promising. For all she knew, Chris might be her future. She should be excited. Maybe that's what the pit in her stomach was...excitement. Definitely.

However, by the time she got home from work, took the dogs out, and ate dinner, she sat on her couch just staring at her phone. She'd already added Chris to her contacts and had a blank text window open, but she was hesitating over what to say.

"What do you think, guys?"

Mr. Muffins cocked his head and then trotted over from his spot in his little bed. Dolly didn't seem inclined to problem solve at the moment. Instead, she selected a toy from her basket and settled down to chew on it.

Patrice reached down and scratched Mr. Muffins behind his ears. He didn't offer any words of wisdom, but she did feel supported by her little fuzzy guy.

Once the scritchies were out of the way, Patrice sighed and got to texting. Short and sweet seemed the way to go. It looked a little abrupt, but she didn't know what else she could say.

Patrice: Hi Chris. This is Patrice, Ashley's friend. How's it going?

She didn't know how long she'd need to wait for a response, but it turned out Chris got back to her within ten minutes.

Chris: Hi Patrice! Nice to 'meet' you. Do you want to grab a bite after work next week?

Patrice: Sounds great. What do you have in mind?

It continued as a bare bones conversation, how could it be

anything else when it was just texting with a stranger? But it was decided that they'd meet for dinner at six o'clock the following Friday night. Chris had insisted that the location should be 'lady's choice' which Patrice thought was nice. She'd asked about any dietary restrictions, because that was just good manners, and they'd agreed to meet at her favorite Mexican place.

The logistics out of the way, they signed off and Patrice exhaled deeply. "That wasn't so bad, was it?"

Mr. Muffins ignored her this time, but Dolly lifted her head just in case the question was about treats or a walk. She looked so cute with her little ears lifted in attention, and her eyes so wide with interest, that Patrice got up to get treats for both dogs.

If only she could muster a fraction of the enthusiasm for her impending date as Mr. Muffins and Dolly had for their treats. Oh well. There was time to get excited. That would kick in closer to the actual date.

No doubt about it.

Surely.

Chapter 4

Tuesday, July 28

There were only three more days until the date with Chris. Although it hadn't been easy, Patrice had gotten herself down to thinking about Seth maybe once or twice a day instead of all day every day. She couldn't help glancing at the park bench he'd sat on when she first saw him, whenever she took the dogs there for a walk, but that was just being aware of her surroundings. She absolutely was not hoping to find him sitting there, waiting to tell her that Julie and Jeremy had eloped and moved to Madagascar to study lemurs. Nope. That wasn't going through her mind at all. Instead, she had much more important things to consider, like what she would wear to meet Chris. In just a few days.

Patrice sat on her bed staring into her open closet, willing inspiration (and excitement) to strike. This was her blue sky she was thinking about, after all. But who was she fooling? Blue skies was Seth's thing anyway. She wouldn't even have thought of it without him. Why did this have to be so horrible?

She closed her eyes to try and block out all thoughts of Seth, but was interrupted from her mental purge by the sound of her dogs going frantic. They started barking like mad and ran to the front door.

That was unusual enough to get her attention. She hurried out of her room to see what had caused them so much angst. They continued barking at her feet so she looked through the peephole on her door. There was nothing to see.

"Hey doggies, chill out. What's gotten into you?"

Afraid they would bolt if she opened the door, she managed to settle them with chewies in their crates. They didn't tend to get upset like that for no reason so she opened her door and discovered an envelope on the floor with her name on it. She picked it up, instinctively running her hand over the messing handwriting before stepping back into her apartment and shutting the door. She unlatched the crate doors, even though the dogs were happily munching, and sat down on the couch. Her fingers tore into the envelope with nearly as much gusto as the dogs with their treats, and found a short, handwritten note. With pounding heart, she read:

Patrice,

I hope you're doing well. To be honest, I'm kind of a mess. I feel terrible about the whole situation and I really want to talk to you. Stupidly, I never got your number. (Told you I wasn't good with girls.) I don't know if you ever want to see me again, but I'm going to be at the Cozy Nook Coffee Shop from 6-7pm this Friday. I hope you'll consider coming. Please. But I'll understand if you don't, and I won't bother you again.

Hope to see you soon,

Chapter 4

Seth

A squeal of delight sprang from her throat before she could even think of it. If that wasn't a telling reaction, she didn't know what was. She jumped up, with the half-formed idea that she should tear out of her apartment, screaming Seth's name, and see if she could find him before he disappeared again, but the impulse was closely followed by silently cursing Seth. Friday at six was her date with Chris. Why did this whole thing have to be so difficult? Surely, that was a sign, right? Good things didn't come easily, but this was all hardship: from dog pee, to a cheating ex, to a double-booked date. One unfortunate obstacle for every meeting? That didn't bode well. The facts still remained. She couldn't be with Seth without becoming tied up with Jeremy again. There was no way around it. As much she liked her Madagascar fantasy, it was just that. Pure fantasy. Reality was that Seth was close with his sisters, which was admirable. Had Julie found herself any other man to marry, Patrice might have even relished the idea of double dates and the promise of fitting in with a fun and loving family. But Julie hadn't. Patrice didn't see how she could ever feel comfortable around Jeremy, and why should she have to? There was too much angst and awkwardness running through the whole impossible situation. She could not go to the surprise meeting with Seth. As much as she wanted to see him again, what good would it do? It'd just be another painful reminder of the man she wanted to get to know better but couldn't.

She couldn't go, and that was that. Although she'd feel like crap for standing him up, he still hadn't given her his number! It's not like she could send him a polite explanation of why she wouldn't be there. Maybe she could have Emily show up and give him a message of her own? Too complicated. Maybe he'd be at the coffee shop a little early and she could swing by first, explain quickly, and then dash off to meet Chris? No. That was even worse.

She sighed and looked over the note in her hands again. Seth had been holding this note in his hands too. It was sort of like holding hands with a ghost. In a desperate, silly move, she quickly kissed his signature and folded the note back up. She popped it into the envelope, got up, and placed it in the drawer of her nightstand. So she wanted to keep it close to her while she slept. Sad? Yes. But sometimes that's just the way things go.

An idea entered her head. What if Seth had gone to the park after dropping off the note? It was so close, it made sense, didn't it?

Without thinking about it anymore than that, Patrice changed into a rayon sundress with a lemon pattern. She didn't feel like slathering her face with sunscreen so she grabbed her wide-brimmed sun hat instead.

"Anybody want to go for a walk?"

Eight little feet skittered to her side, jumping and hopping in anticipation.

She made sure both collars and leashes were firmly secured and headed out for a totally random walk in the park.

It was warmer than a hot, buttered biscuit outside. In fact, she could probably bake some in a pan on the sidewalk. The air had a distinct oven-y quality to it, but she pressed on. She'd already committed to a walk in the park. Might as well go through with it. Even though she quickly realized she should have grabbed a cold bottle of water before she'd left. Oops.

She and the dogs were already drooping by the time they made it to the park but she couldn't stop herself. Even though she knew better, she just had to see for herself.

When they made it to the shade of the tree-lined portion of the path, the slightly cooler air was a tiny relief.

In an act of rebellion, Mr. Muffins and Dolly both stopped walking and stood, panting, in the grass.

The mini-coup brought Patrice back to her rapidly overheating senses.

"Come on, guys." She pointed up ahead another fifteen feet or so. "Let's get up to the water fountain for a drink and then we'll go back home. Okay?"

The dogs followed her finger with their heads but their little bodies remained rooted to the spot.

Patrice scooped them up, one under each arm, and carried them to the fountain. She took turns holding them up to the water and letting them drink before getting a long drink of her own.

From the fountain, she could see 'Seth's bench,' which was empty. She tried to ignore that the sight made her heart melt down into the soles of her feet. Of course he wasn't there. Why would he sit out in the blistering heat on the off chance she'd show up with the dogs? That was the sort of thing that happened in the movies. Not real life. Definitely not Patrice's life. He'd dropped off a letter for her. What more could she expect…from a man she was going to stand up anyway?

She sighed and headed back home.

With any luck, she'd get home, take a cold shower, and forget everything besides meeting Chris for dinner. Maybe she'd even convince herself to daydream about what he'd be like instead of remembering details about Seth. Like how he looked away so adorably when he smiled. Wait. No. She wasn't thinking about that. She was thinking about dinner with Chris. After all, he could turn out to be 'the one.' Wouldn't Ashley love that? They could all laugh and reminisce together about how Patrice had asked to be set up and Ashley had immediately come through with the love of her life. Yep. That's how it was going to work out. She convinced herself of it as she stood in the same spot in the shower where Seth's own bare feet had been a couple weeks earlier.

Chapter 5

Friday, July 31

"What are you wearing?"

Once again, Patrice had her phone on speaker, staring into the closet with Emily on the line.

"I was thinking I couldn't go wrong with a little black dress, right?"

A rumble of thunder and a flash of lightning answered her before Emily did.

"Classic and clean, yes, but it won't show much of your personality."

"But can't he figure that out when he talks to me?" Patrice fingered the hem of her black dress, not even feeling convinced that it was the right choice.

"Yes, but it's fun to knock them out with it all in one glance."

"I don't even like dressing up when it's raining. My legs get all wet and then I freeze in the air conditioning the whole time. Maybe I'll play it casual and just wear jeans and a blouse. That will give him a healthy dose of my personality."

"It's kinda hot for jeans though. Even if it's raining."

Emily had a point. The heat wave had not let up at all. The rain wasn't really cooling things down either. It was more of a steamy, jungle rain than a cooling rain.

"Okay. I'll wear my lemon skirt with a white blouse."

"You might want to rethink a white blouse in the rain."

"Good catch." Patrice pushed past the white blouse and pulled out a navy blue one instead. It wasn't quite as cute as the white one but she didn't want to risk giving everyone a peep show with their dinner.

With her ensemble sorted out, Patrice gave herself a once over in the full-length mirror. She didn't want to wear sandals, because of the rain, so she opted for a pair of no-show socks with white canvas sneakers. She was definitely rocking a casual/quirky vibe but that was consistent with her personality. At least Chris would know right off the bat that he wasn't dining with a high maintenance girl.

She didn't want to mess around with much makeup either. She set her phone on the counter and went for a fresh-faced look with a light pink lipstick and a neutral eye. Good enough.

"Are you excited?"

Patrice blotted her lipstick and gave her reflection a final glance. She tilted the phone to get a look at the time. 5:35. It made her body prickle with sweaty anxiety, the same way she felt before giving a presentation.

"Uh, yeah. Of course I'm excited. Chris could be the one, right? That would be fun." She walked back into her room to grab her purse. Her eyes slid to her nightstand, causing her heart to pound even more ferociously. Was Seth feeling as nervous as she was as he wondered if she'd show up or not?

"Well, you don't have to put that kind of pressure on it. Just have fun." Emily's voice of reason gave her something to ground herself with.

"Yeah. Fun. I think it will be fun. Chris sounds like a nice guy."

"Patrice?"

"Hmm?" Patrice did a quick scan of her bedroom, to make sure she wasn't forgetting anything vital she should bring.

"Why are you suddenly talking like a robot?"

"I'm not!"

"Fun. Yes. Chris will be fun. Define 'fun,'" Emily said in a staccato robot voice.

Patrice laughed nervously. She hadn't told Emily or Ashley about Seth's letter. It was hard enough to process on her own. She didn't think she could handle any additional input on that matter.

"It's a blind date. I may be a little nervous."

"Nothing to worry about," Emily assured her. "Just be your wonderful self and have a good time. Ashley has good taste. She wouldn't set you up with someone unless she thought they were genuinely worthy."

Patrice's phone pinged with a new text.

"Thanks, Em. Someone's texting me. It might be Chris. I better go. I'll let you know how it goes."

"K. Have fun! Bye!"

Patrice ended the call and looked at the text. It was from Ashley.

"Good luck! Hope you have a great time. Fingers crossed!"

"Thx. Leaving now." Patrice replied and then slipped her phone into her purse. She couldn't stand anymore pre-socializing socializing. Her heart was thumping like she'd give herself a heart attack. Not because of Chris. She couldn't stop visualizing Seth sitting alone at the coffee house, hoping she'd show up. That was the word he'd used himself, 'hope.'

She wasn't the kind of person who stood up other people.

She got the dogs crated for her date and caught a glimpse of her wall clock. It was already 5:40. If she didn't get going, she'd be standing up two men in one night. With the rain pouring down like that, it'd probably take her twenty or twenty-five minutes to get to the Mexican place.

But a thought popped into her head and she ran to her jewelry box for one quick accessory: the Eiffel tower bracelet she hadn't worn in ages. She took it out and fastened it on her wrist. She wasn't sure why she'd done it, but seeing it again made her smile. Then it was time to go!

Feeling like she was running on fight or flight impulses, she donned her raincoat, dashed out of her building, and ran across the parking lot to her car. Just before she got to it, she accidentally splashed through a puddle, soaking her canvas shoes through to her feet. Nice. Now she'd have swampfoot for the remainder of her evening. But it was too late to go back and change now. She was already cutting it too close as it was.

She jumped into the car and put the heat on full blast from the floor vents. It wouldn't really dry her feet out, but made her feel like she was doing something.

She tuned the radio to the classical station, hoping it would help lower her blood pressure as she drove. Her nerves were so heightened she might as well be driving in the Grand Prix.

It wasn't until she stopped for a red light that she realized Cozy Nook Coffee House was on her way to the restaurant. She could see the glow of its sign through her rain-streaked windows. Her heavy breathing quickly fogged up the glass until she had to wipe it away with her hand.

Thoughts crashed into her skull like a roller-skating elephant. Was Seth waiting for her in there at that very moment? Was he sipping a latte trying to pretend he wasn't terrified that she wouldn't show?

She practically pressed her nose to the glass trying to squint enough to see through the front window. Was that brownish blur Seth's wavy hair?

The car behind her laid on the horn, jolting Patrice back to attention. She slammed her foot on the gas, launching the car forward. So much for the soothing power of classical music.

She pulled herself together to concentrate on driving safely, even though her intense heart rate didn't let up a bit. With every beat, her brain seemed to think, Seth, Seth, Seth right along with it.

She made it to the restaurant and glanced at her clock. Only five minutes late. She pulled out her phone and sent Chris a quick text: Just pulled in. I'll be right there.

She tucked her phone back into her purse and took a deep breath. The rain was still pounding down relentlessly. She reached back and pulled up the hood on her raincoat. If the heater had done anything to dry out her shoes, it was all about to be lost on her dash into the restaurant. She should have just gone for jeans and regular sneakers. At least she would have been more comfortable.

Her phone pinged with a new message as she put her hand on the door handle. Might as well check it first. She fished her phone back out of her purse and saw Chris's message. "Be careful. It's intense out there. Did you bring an umbrella? I can come out and get you if you'd like."

Her heart settled down a bit. That was sweet of him. Ashley

had come through. Chris was a gentleman. Better yet, his sister wasn't going to marry her ex. She needed to give him a chance.

She texted back that that was sweet, but unnecessary. Then she put her phone away again and ran for it. Her feet seemed to find every puddle in the parking lot and her socks slopped against her soles making a lovely squelching sound as she walked into the restaurant. Soaked to the bone, she stood dripping in the entry of the restaurant. As predicted, the air conditioning was like a blast chiller on her bare, wet skin. Her glasses fogged up instantly. It was going to be a long dinner.

"Patrice?"

She took off her glasses to wipe away the steam with the bottom of her shirt, making herself momentarily blind in the process. With most of the fog wiped away, she put them back on and peered into the friendly blue eyes of an attractive young man.

"Yes. You must be Chris?"

"I am." His eyes roamed from her face, down to her feet and back. Not in a sleazy way. He was just taking in the sorry state of her. "You're soaked to the skin. I should have come out to meet you."

Patrice took in the sight of this guy who she'd been trying to imagine. He was attractive, but not in the way she was expecting. He had a smooth, shaved head but it complemented his features. He had kind but piercing eyes. His mouth was set off with a small blonde goatee. Whereas Seth's face was round and soft, Chris's was more chiseled and angular. Patrice inhaled deeply and immediately remembered what Ashley had said about him. There was a sweet, earthy scent about him that was very pleasant. He was wearing a blue button-down shirt with a pair of black jeans. His vibe was chic but comfortable. Patrice probably wouldn't have picked him out for herself but she could certainly see the appeal.

Patrice shrugged. "I thought my raincoat would do a little more for me. It's ok. I'll dry out." The fact that she'd dry out eventually did nothing to quell the goosebumps that the air conditioning was already raising on her arms and legs.

Chris looked at her, a little unsure.

Patrice decided to channel her nerves into friendliness and get on with things.

"It's nice to finally meet you."

"It is." Chris snapped back to himself, apparently prepared to commit to the date if she was too. "Our table is this way." He held out his arm to indicate that their table was on the right side of the restaurant.

"Lead the way." She was grateful to have Chris's eyes off her for a moment as she tried to shake out her skirt a little, but it was no use. It was so wet it just clung to her legs in a less than modest manner. So much for casual cute. She was sporting the drowned rat look.

Chris gestured to their booth and she squeaked her way onto the seat. She could cross 'ladylike' off the list of possible first impressions.

"I got us both a glass of ice water." Chris kindly ignored the rude noises a wet body sliding over vinyl seating makes. "I didn't know what you'd want."

As if on cue, the waitress strode over.

"Is water okay for you, miss?"

"I'll take a Coke please, and could I put in an appetizer?" She looked at Chris to see his reaction.

He nodded encouragingly. "Whatever you'd like."

"Could we start with a baked avocado, please?" Her mouth

started watering just thinking about it. She may be sopping wet, but at least she knew the meal would be excellent.

"Of course. Coke and a baked avocado. Anything else for you to drink, sir?"

"I'll also take a Coke. Thanks."

The waitress moved off leaving Chris to smile at Patrice for the first time. "Baked avocado sounds delicious."

"It's incredible. If you like avocado at all, you'll love this. It's life-changingly good."

Chris leaned forward in his seat. "Wow. That's quite an endorsement. I'm excited to try this."

Patrice took a sip of her water, as though she needed any further hydration at the moment. She could have gone for a hot drink. Like a coffee. Her mind didn't hesitate to remind her that Seth was sitting down the road in a coffee shop at that moment. Even if he'd gotten drenched in the process, he was probably enjoying a hot drink. Maybe even a bowl of soup or a warm brownie.

Patrice was sorely tempted to pull out her phone and see what time it was, but she knew that would be supremely rude. She was honoring her dinner date with Chris. She had to stop the madness.

"That's a pretty bracelet." Chris gestured toward Patrice's wrist, which he'd gotten a good look at while she was drinking. "Have you been to Paris?"

"Oh, thanks." Patrice was pleased he'd noticed it, but also felt a little shy that she'd worn it again after all this time. Must have been because of her conversation with Seth. "I haven't actually been there. My high school friend and I were in French class together and I got this to remember her. I hope to visit there someday, but I don't think my French is nearly as good as it was then."

"I'm not in touch with any of my high school friends anymore either. Funny isn't it? At the time, it feels like you'll be best friends forever, but in reality, it doesn't take too long to drift apart. Sort of like those high school language classes. You think four years of practice will stick with you, but that goes away too."

Chris took a sip of his water and Patrice averted her gaze to the little Eiffel tower charm dangling from her bracelet.

She didn't feel like sharing the reason she and Mariah were no longer in touch. It just didn't feel natural so she changed the subject.

"So, Ashley told me you're in marketing. I do graphic design for an ad agency, so we do similar sort of work."

"Yeah. Ashley told me you were in graphic design. What kind of clients do you work with?"

They both exchanged polite work conversation until the waitress brought the Cokes over. They both took a quick sip and then chuckled at each other.

Chris jumped in to lead the next topic of conversation.

"So, do you have any hobbies? What do you like to do for fun?"

"Well, I have two Pomeranians that keep me busy. We take lots of walks and watch movies together. My friend, Emily, is in an Irish folk music band and I like to go to her shows. How about you?"

"I love the great outdoors. When I'm not working, I like to spend long weekends backpacking and camping. My goal is to hike the Appalachian Trail one day."

"Wow. That's an incredible goal." Patrice was already out of her depth. She was the opposite of outdoorsy and woefully ignorant of the Appalachian Trail. She knew it must be long because she'd heard of people wanting to hike it all, but she had no frame of reference. "Forgive my ignorance. How long is the trail?"

Chris's face lit right up just thinking about it.

"It's nearly 2,200 miles long. But to put that in perspective, it can take five to seven months to hike straight through."

"Five to seven months?" Patrice was certainly not equipped to be a hiking partner with a person like Chris. She got winded if she had to take two flights of stairs.

"It takes a lot of preparation to get ready for a hike like that."

"I can't even imagine! How can anybody keep a job and go for a hike like that? Wouldn't you be scared to lose your livelihood?"

"It's a thrilling tradeoff. I'd be scared to go through my life and never actually hike the trail. I've already started taking some steps to make it happen."

Patrice nodded encouragingly and interjected the appropriate sounds of interest here and there, but her brain sort of faded out of the conversation when he started explaining food drops. To be sure, his enthusiasm was adorable and she didn't mind him talking about his passion. It was just that she wasn't feeling that spark of connection.

She excused herself after the appetizer had been eaten. They couldn't have gotten that plate any cleaner unless they'd licked it. He did agree that the baked avocado was life-changing.

Still soaking wet, Patrice locked herself in a bathroom stall and pulled out her phone. 6:35. Chris was a good guy. There was no denying that, but conversation didn't touch her like it had with Seth. This felt more like an interview.

She weighed her options. The entrees should be out anytime. In fact, they were probably being placed on the table that moment, since meals usually seemed to arrive when someone was in the bathroom. If she wolfed it down in ten minutes, she could pay for her half of the bill and make a run for it. Seth said he'd be at the coffee house until seven. If he was anything like her, he'd hold out hope until the last possible second, wouldn't he? She could stop by, see what he had to say, and then she'd know for sure. What if he did want to tell her that Julie and Jeremy were moving to Madagascar? Or even somewhere less outlandish than that? Out of state. Out of country. That wasn't so far-fetched.

Why had she thought it was a good idea to blow Seth off?

Panic pressed against her chest. She was dangerously close to missing out, but she didn't want to be a jerk to Chris either. He was a very nice man, just not the right man for her.

She hurried back to her seat like her shoes were on fire, even though they were still very squishy and waterlogged. Relief fanned the flames of hope in her heart when she discovered their meals sitting at their places.

Chris, who really was a gentleman, had waited for her to return to start eating his dinner. She took a deep breath and eyed her full plate of delicious tacos de papas. Ten minutes. She had ten minutes to get as much down as she could and figure out a way to get out of there.

"That smells really good." Chris eyed Patrice's plate.

"These are so delicious. Just as amazing as those avocados. Do you want to try one? This is more than enough for me."

"I don't want to be the weirdo who shares food on a first date, but that really has my mouth watering. Are you sure you don't mind?"

"Not at all!" Patrice had never been more willing to share in her life. She quickly scooped up a taco with her spoon and fork and transferred it over to Chris's plate before he could change his mind.

"Do you want to try any of my-"

Patrice shook her head and bit into her first taco. "Trust me. I'll be stuffed after one or two of these. They're very hearty."

The taste sensation exploded on her tongue slowing her down just a bit. She especially loved the flavor combo of the potato hash with the melted muenster. And she couldn't forget that little kick of chipotle cream. It had just enough heat that it made her nose run but didn't burn her throat. It was so good! She'd normally savor each mouthful, but there wasn't time tonight. And she still needed a polite and plausible reason to book it out of there. The clock was ticking.

She polished off two tacos in record time and she could feel her gut straining against the waist of that stupid skirt she never should have worn.

Chris was eating his meal at the pace of a normal human being. Probably slower since she'd placed the burden of conversation on him while she used her mouth for the single purpose of snarfing down her food.

"I always eat too much here." She removed her napkin from her lap and placed it on the table, preparing to make her swift exit. "Everything is so delicious, I can't help myself."

"You're right about that. This place was an excellent choice. I'm really glad you suggested it."

"I'm glad." She reached into her purse to pull out her wallet and steal a sneaky glance at her phone. It was already 6:52! The coffee shop wasn't far away, but getting in the door by seven was impossible. She had to get out of there immediately or she'd lose her chance forever.

She slapped a twenty on the table and decided she had to

make the rudest, most abrupt departure of her life.

"Chris, I have to tell you the truth. This has been fun, but I just realized I was supposed to meet someone else fifteen minutes ago. I can't stand being so rude, but I have to run. I'm so sorry." She stood up, leaving Chris open-mouthed with silent shock.

Turning away, her feet were already sloshing a hasty retreat. She was on the verge of missing Seth and it was suddenly dawning on her how very much she'd regret it if she never spoke to him again. All of the thoughts and memories she'd been trying to repress since the night of the concert crowded into her brain. She didn't even notice her feet getting soaked for the third time as she ran to her car.

The rain had let up somewhat, but it was still a steady downpour rather than the blinding buckets that had come down on the way to meet Chris.

Her foot pressed down on the accelerator harder than was prudent, but she mentally dared any cop to try pulling her over right now. She refused to stop until she got to the coffee shop.

"Please be there. Please be there. Please be there." She repeated her new mantra the whole drive to the shop. She didn't stop when she raced from the car and flung open the door with more force than necessary. It was 7:07 when she stepped into the shop. Surely that was a lucky time if there ever was one. Her eyes swept over the faces of everyone huddled in the shop once…twice…three times.

A barista wandered over from behind the counter, probably alarmed by the wide-eyed panic on Patrice's rain-streaked face.

"Can I help you?"

"I'm looking for a man. I'm late but he was supposed to be here until seven. Oh God. Where is he?"

The poor barista noted the tone of hysteria in Patrice's voice and attempted to combat it with her own most soothing tones.

"Okay, well, could you tell me what he looks like? It's a small place. I might remember him."

"He's kind of stocky. Glasses. Wavy brown hair. His name is Seth and he actually resembles a young Seth Rogen."

The barista's eyes flickered in recognition.

"Yes. He was here, but you literally just missed him. He left maybe a minute or two before you walked in."

"Damn it! Thanks!" Patrice turned on her heel and ran out of the shop, the weight of cosmic desperation pushing down on her.

"Seth!" His name ripped out of her mouth before the door had fully shut behind her. "I'm here! Seth!" She might as well be shouting into the proverbial void. All she got was a few strange looks from people in the parking lot. No sign of Seth.

She whipped her head around like a trapped, wild animal. Surely, he was there somewhere within reach. She hadn't missed him by that much. A minute? Two? That was only one hundred and twenty seconds. Too narrow of a miss to destroy her chance of seeing him again. She wouldn't believe it.

"Seth! Seth!"

Every moving thing caught her eye. Cars passing on the street. Dome lights coming on in cars in the stormy evening. People hurrying to and from buildings. Finally, she caught a glimpse of a big black umbrella disappearing around a corner into a residential area. Were her eyes deceiving her or was there a flash of blue under that umbrella?

"Seth!" She shouted to be heard over the never-ending hum and splashing of the cars going down the main road. "Wait Seth! I'm coming!"

She took off running, paying attention to nothing other than where she'd seen the umbrella disappear. Her sodden shoes flopped heavily against her feet. They were so heavy with water they moved against her strides rather than with them. She kicked them off and kept running in her socks.

She rounded the corner where she might have seen Seth and looked down the sidewalk before her. Sure enough, there was a stocky man with his head under a black umbrella. It could definitely be Seth.

"Seth!"

Finally, the umbrella toting stranger stopped and turned to face her.

With her hair streaming into her eyes with the rain, she practically burst into tears at the sight of him.

Without thinking, she ran to him, splashing through puddles that were deeper than they looked.

When she finally reached him, she was so wet and grateful she didn't care anymore. She threw her arms around him and finally hugged him tight.

"I'm so sorry I'm late," she cried into his shoulder.

"Are you okay? You're absolutely soaked and are those…I mean…where are your shoes?" Seth wrapped his arms around Patrice but angled his head to stare down the soggy length of her.

"I was so stupid," she said. "I thought I could stop thinking about you, but I was wrong. I haven't stopped thinking about you since the day we met. I didn't think I could face you again because of stupid Jeremy, but I was wrong about that too."

"Hey, it's okay." Seth rested his head against Patrice's. "I'm glad you caught me."

Now that she'd found him, the panicky pounding of her heart subsided into a more normal rhythm for the first time that evening.

"Seriously though, what happened to your shoes?"

Patrice stepped back from the embrace and laughed at her own absurd state. "I've been through a lot of puddles tonight."

"I guess so. You look like you've been swimming."

Their arms still loosely holding on to each other, they found themselves face to face. The mirth faded from their eyes as something more deep and serious took hold.

Patrice looked close at the beauty of Seth's brown eyes so close to hers. She could see darker little freckles in his irises and even some golden lines. Suddenly, she knew very clearly what she wanted. Sharing the safety of Seth's secret blue skies umbrella, she leaned in. Their lips were like two gravitational fields that pulled relentlessly at each other until the distance was crossed and they kissed.

Patrice no longer felt the cold weight of her wet clothes or the hard concrete sidewalk under her stocking feet. All she felt was the plump smoothness of Seth's lips and the warmth of his tongue as it flirted with hers.

The sound of the rain faded into the background as her ears tuned into Seth's breath and the tiniest groan of pleasure that escaped his throat as they kissed. It was everything a dramatic rain kiss should be and it was actually happening!

When they pulled apart, Seth stared at her in wonder.

"Wow. I wasn't expecting that."

"Me neither. But I sure don't regret it."

"No, no. I don't either, but maybe we should talk before we do that again. Assuming you'd want to do that again." Seth's cheeks got a little pinker as self-consciousness crept over him.

Patrice took the opportunity to run her thumb over his lips, gently trying to smudge off the lipstick she'd left there.

"I'd very much like to do that again."

Seth swallowed drily, and Patrice could see his Adam's apple bobbing.

"Ok. We're in agreement there, but first, your shoes and my place." He looked down the sidewalk behind her, hoping to see shoes somewhere and then glanced behind him gauging how far they were from his house.

"You live here?" Patrice was pleasantly surprised that Seth lived in a neighborhood, before she suddenly wondered if he lived with his parents, or worse yet, his sister.

"Yeah. I got a place a year after I got my job. Didn't want to spend rent money when I could put it into my own house instead. I'm seven houses down from here. Want me to drop you off there and I can come back for your shoes?"

With Seth right in front of her again, she could care less about the shoes, but she supposed it wasn't very good to be a litterbug.

"I could live without the shoes."

Seth put his arm tentatively around Patrice's waist and started heading toward his house. "I can get the shoes."

Patrice was surprised how comfortable it felt to have Seth's arm around her and she slung hers low across his back too. She'd thought she might never see him again, and now they were strolling through a downpour together. There was no way of knowing what he wanted to talk to her about, but given the loss she'd felt since the concert, she was happy to enjoy the moment with him.

They walked up the steps of his cute little bungalow and she held the umbrella while he fished out his keys and unlocked the front door.

A stocky little brown and white bulldog perked up, caught sight of Patrice and started to bark.

"Pierre, stop it. We have a guest." Seth gave Patrice a little squeeze to demonstrate to Pierre that she was a welcome addition to the house.

Patrice stepped inside and instantly fell in love with that smooshy little face. She dropped to her knees and beckoned the wary creature to come be friends.

"Pierre," she cooed. "You're absolutely beautiful. Do you know that? Do you know how beautiful you are?"

Seth stifled a chuckle, still standing in the doorway.

Pierre approached Patrice with caution and gingerly sniffed her fingertips. He pressed his nose into her hands for a thorough inspection. When he finally finished, he sneezed, shook his head, and then allowed her to pet his head.

"Oh, who's a good boy? Do you know who the good boy is? It's you, isn't it! You're a good boy, Pierre. Yes, you are."

"I think he's going to like you more than he likes me."

"Nobody loves his daddy more than you do. Isn't that right, Pierre? Yes, you do love your daddy. Yes, you do!" Patrice had already gotten Pierre to flop down onto his back and beg for belly rubs, which she was all too happy to give.

Seth cleared his throat. "Pierre isn't being a very good host. You're soaked to the bone. I guess the tables have turned. You can wear some of my clothes and I'll dry yours."

"Wow. I guess we've already come full circle." Patrice gave Pierre a final tummy rub and stood up. Her clothes were definitely too wet to just hang out in. Way worse now than when she'd had dinner with Chris.

"I'll go put something out for you in my room. You can get changed while I go find your shoes."

Seth disappeared into his bedroom to find something that might fit her okay. He was definitely larger than her so he found a pair of old sweatpants, from when he was a little thinner, that had a drawstring waist. Hopefully, she could pull them tight enough to stay up. He also selected a t-shirt he thought might make her smile. He spread the outfit out on his bed and went back out to get her.

"Everything's on the bed for you. But if it doesn't fit, feel free to rifle around in the closet and see if you can find something better. I don't have any skeletons in there. Promise."

Patrice was loving this already. Even in another crazy circumstance, it was easier and more comfortable to talk with Seth than it had been with Chris.

"Thank you. I won't uncover any secrets while you're gone. But really, don't look too hard. I'll be fine without the shoes."

"Ah, but it's a matter of honor now. Never fear. Your shoes will reappear!"

Patrice laughed. It was so silly, but insanely endearing, and she couldn't help thinking that she wanted to kiss him again. Very soon. But Seth turned, gave Pierre instructions to take care of the lady while he was gone, and disappeared back into the rain to find her missing sneakers.

Now that her adrenaline and nervous energy were wearing off, the chill of the wet, clingy clothes were making their presence known. She squished her way into Seth's room and surveyed the outfit he'd left for her. She also took in Seth's bedroom. He had a very comfy looking queen-sized bed with blue and white striped sheets. He definitely wasn't playing house. There was a matching bedroom set complete with nightstands and a dresser. It also appeared that he was a very neat person. No piles of dirty clothes anywhere, but there was a dog bed at the foot of the bed.

She pushed her skirt down her legs and let it slop in a heap at her feet. Unfortunately, her underwear was also soaked, so she rolled that down and it transformed into a twisted wet rope by the time it got to her ankles. She may feel comfortable with Seth, but she wasn't about to wear his underwear. Not that she thought it was cool to go commando in his pants either, but she had to do something. Commando it was.

Her blouse had been protected by the rain jacket, but the bottom of it was wet from the skirt so she took that off too.

First, she pulled on the sweats, but they hung dangerously low on her hips. One false move and they'd be laying on the ground. In some circumstances, that wouldn't be a bad thing, but as much as she was attracted to Seth, it was way too soon for that. She tugged the drawstring as tight as it would go and the waistband almost clung to her hips. Good enough.

She considered tucking in the tee shirt to add a little more bulk to shore up the pants but didn't want to look that ridiculous. Instead, she let the Mr. Sunshine shirt he'd set out hang down to her mid-thigh. Wearing Seth's clothes made her feel like a tiny pixie girl and she hugged herself tight, imagining how the fabric had once clung to Seth's body.

Gathering up her bundle of wet clothes, she waddled out of Seth's room, so her pants would stay up. She didn't want to go snooping through his whole house to find his washer and dryer, but she did locate the bathroom to drop her clothes in the tub. A furry little shadow followed her from Seth's room, to the bathroom, back to the living room, where she made herself comfortable on the couch. Pierre jumped right up beside her and stared at her with the mournful eyes of a dog who wants to convey how neglected he is without constant petting.

She gathered his droopy face in her hands and booped his nose with her own, prompting him to give her kisses.

Patrice was just about to launch into another baby talk round of praise for good boy, Pierre, when the door opened and Seth returned with the wayward, waterlogged shoes.

"I feel like the prince who found the glass slipper, except canvas is so much more practical. Although, I suppose glass would be waterproof." He cocked his head like he was really weighing the merit of glass slippers in a rainstorm.

Patrice took a break from smooshing Pierre's face to thank Seth.

"You are certainly a valiant prince for going back into the rainstorm to retrieve my shoes. Thank you."

"I see you're changed into something dry. Did you ransack the place looking for the dryer?"

"No. I got distracted by Mr. Cutie Face here and left my wet stuff in the tub. I can get it-"

Seth held up his hands. "I can see that 'Mr. Cutie Face' has fallen in love with you. You two stay here and snuggle. I'll get your clothes in the dryer, for a change."

Seth went off to handle the domestic work, leaving Patrice and Pierre to continue bonding. She had also given a cursory glance around the house and found that, for a bachelor pad, it was tidy and comfortable. There was a glowing, pulsating light emanating from an impressive computer setup in the corner of the room, and a large flatscreen television hooked up to three different video game systems. IT was definitely where Seth belonged. It was clearly a major part of his life, at work and at home.

When Seth came back, he took a seat in his recliner, across from the couch. Leaning his elbows on his knees, he exhaled a big breath. The glint of mischief had faded from his eyes.

Patrice turned her attention away from Pierre and could feel the energy of the room go serious. She'd had her dramatic gesture of running through the rain to get to Seth, now it was time to let him say what was on his mind.

"So." Patrice tucked her rain-bedraggled hair behind her ears. "What did you want to talk to me about?"

Seth looked down at the floor, gathering his thoughts for a moment, before he boldly looked her in the eye.

"I wanted to let you know that some things have happened since we last saw each other."

His tone wasn't cold, but the words caused Patrice to sit up a little straighter, as if she was in an important work meeting and about to receive some harsh news. She nodded for him to go on.

Seth bit his lip for a moment before he decided to just continue on with it.

"I did tell Julie about you and Jeremy. She's my sister, I have to look out for her. If Jeremy wasn't willing to tell her about what he'd done in the past, I was. She'd agreed to marry the guy. She deserved to know."

The words washed over Patrice like a cold wave. Well, the truth was out. Everyone in their bizarrely connected circle was on the same page now. She couldn't imagine what the fallout would have been from a revelation like that.

"How did that go?"

Seth puffed out his cheeks then blew out a long breath.

"Probably about as well as you expect it to. Julie was shocked. Then she was horrified for herself and for you. She couldn't stand that you'd been thinking of her as a trashy man-stealer all this time and she and Jeremy had a huge fight."

Patrice sucked in her breath. Even though Jeremy had hurt her with his behavior, she didn't like the feeling that she could jeopardize his future. Suddenly, all the revenge scenarios she'd envisioned back at the time, seemed shallow and counterproductive. She just wanted him to live his life, out of range of her and her own life. Was that too much to ask?

"What happened?"

"It was a tense week, I can tell you that. It was a lot for Julie to process. She felt bad for herself, she felt bad for you and me too. We had a lot of tough conversations but a couple of important things emerged from all that."

Patrice just stared at Seth, holding her breath, pulse racing once again. She couldn't bring herself to speak.

"Julie and Jeremy are still together and still getting married. And I realized that even though we haven't known each other long, I kinda feel like I've known you forever. It seems like you get me and I don't find that with many people. I know the Julie and Jeremy thing is awkward and uncomfortable and I wish it wasn't like that, but I want to keep going with what we started. Even if you only want to be friends. Would you be okay with that?"

Patrice's lips trembled from the emotion she was holding in. She shook her head and got up to kneel in front of Seth.

"You're too cute to just be friends with. Besides, I just discovered what an amazing kisser you are. I could use a lot more of that in my life, please. I don't want to take a romantic relationship off the table, if that's okay with you."

Seth collapsed back into his chair and looked up at the ceiling with a huge smile on his face.

"Are you for real?" He peered down the length of his body at her. "It's incredible that we both feel that way for each other, but what about the Jeremy thing? As much as I would like to just kiss you again right now and forget all that drama, shouldn't we talk this out a little? It seems like we should have some strategy."

He was so introspective and mature her heart was doing backflips of joy inside her chest.

"You're so sensible." She sat back on her heels and wondered how she ever thought she could walk away from those deep brown eyes forever. Jeremy had hurt her once, but letting Seth go was just hurting herself.

"I guess it's going to take some work, from all four of us." Patrice picked at the hem of her shirt while she thought it out. "Julie and Jeremy are getting married, but does she really want to have Jeremy's ex around? That can't be a whole lot of fun for her either."

Doubt began to creep in again. It was going to take more than a delicious kiss to make this situation right, no matter how much Seth and Patrice liked each other.

"Julie and I have probably talked more seriously in the past week than we have our entire lives. She walked through all the angles she could think of and her bottom line was this. She thought you were fun and nice at the concert, before she knew your history with Jeremy. She said I was a 'lighter, brighter' person after I met you in the park and she liked that about you immediately. She's willing to concentrate on the person in front of her rather than her imaginings of the past and she'll support us if we want to be together. She also said she'd love to hang out with you sometime, just the girls, if that's ok with you."

If she'd learned anything from trying to forget about Seth, it was that she desperately wanted to know all about him. It might be a weird road ahead, but she was ready to buckle up and see where it led.

"I want to see where it'll go." Patrice slipped her hands into Seth's and gently tugged him forward to sit on the floor with her.

"I do too." He mirrored her cross-legged position, sitting knee to knee with her. "You think you'll be able to stand it?"

Patrice had an image of going out to lunch with Julie to just talk. It didn't sound like a whole lot of fun, but she hadn't thought she could talk Tyree into using one of her original designs for Gilmore and look how that turned out.

"It'll definitely be weird at first," Patrice mused. "But I think you're worth it."

Seth's cheeks turned a shade of pink and he closed his eyes as he absorbed the weight of the compliment.

Just as he was leaning forward to indulge in another kiss, Patrice put her fingers to his lips. "Before this goes any further, there's one thing I need to do."

Seth opened his eyes in surprise and Patrice dashed over to the couch to grab her phone from her purse.

"This time, I have to get your number!"

About the Author

Alana Oxford is a Michigan author of romcoms, sweet romance, and humorous women's fiction. She wants her stories to bring sunshine and smiles to her readers. She enjoys improv comedy, moody music, everything book related, and has an ongoing love affair with the United Kingdom.

If you enjoyed this book, please let others know by leaving a review on your favorite websites. A few minutes sharing your thoughts means so much to authors and helps them find potential readers. Thank you in advance for sharing the book love!

*Author photo credit: Arace Photographic

You can connect with me on:

🐦 https://twitter.com/AlanaOxford

📘 https://www.facebook.com/AlanaOxford

📷 https://instagram.com/alanaoxford

Subscribe to my newsletter:

✉ https://mailchi.mp/c11fca6b5494/alana-oxford-newsletter-signup

Also by Alana Oxford

Forthcoming titles:

Librarian in Love series

My Modern Midlife Crisis

Made in the USA
Monee, IL
04 June 2021